A RISKY GAME

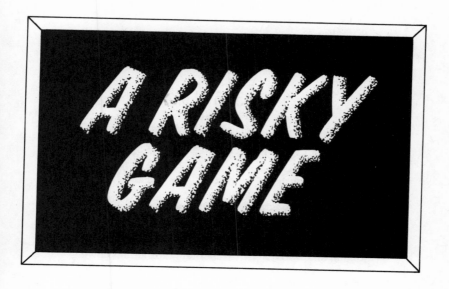

A RISKY GAME

STEPHEN SCHWANDT

HENRY HOLT AND COMPANY
NEW YORK

505710.X

Published by Henry Holt and Company, Inc.
521 Fifth Avenue, New York, New York 10175.
Published simultaneously in Canada.

Library of Congress Cataloging in Publication Data
Schwandt, Stephen.
A risky game.
Summary: A teacher draws Julie, a student, into
joining him in staging a psychodrama for an unknowing
senior English class, purportedly to study the students'
reactions, but events become painful, frightening, and
complicated, and Julie questions the choices she has
made and the teacher's motives.
[1. Teachers—Fiction. 2. High schools—Fiction.
3. Schools—Fiction. 4. Psychology—Fiction] I. Title.
PZ7.S39955Ri   1986   [Fic]   86-9860
ISBN: 0-8050-0091-7

First Edition

Designed by Jeffrey L. Ward
Printed in the United States of America
1 3 5 7 9 10 8 6 4 2

The author gratefully acknowledges permission to reprint
an excerpt from *Rosencrantz and Guildenstern Are Dead* by
Tom Stoppard, copyright © 1967 by Tom Stoppard.
Reprinted by permission of Grove Press, Inc.

ISBN 0-8050-0091-7

For the C.A.S.T.
And for Special K, with love

GUILDENSTERN: We only know what we're told, and that's little enough. And for all we know it isn't even true.

THE PLAYER: Everything has to be taken on trust; truth is only that which is taken to be true.

GUILDENSTERN: It's a matter of asking the right questions and giving away as little as we can. It's a game.

—Tom Stoppard, *Rosencrantz and Guildenstern Are Dead*

A RISKY GAME

CHAPTER
1

"Juliet, did I ever tell you about . . ." He paused for effect, then whispered, ". . . the Phantom?"

Julie shook her head, a curious half-smile forming as she anticipated yet another combat story from the endless war between the Westpark High School faculty and students.

"Can I trust you with this one, Miss Lamar? I mean, if anyone finds out . . ."

"Sure." She nodded. He always prefaced the best of his inside anecdotes with that line, but she knew it was a rhetorical question. She knew Mr. Conner trusted her, although she wasn't quite sure why. And she wasn't at all sure how they'd become such good friends in so short a time. By now, when they talked she didn't feel like she was talking to a teacher. Troy Conner often seemed like an older, wiser, more experienced brother. A father figure sometimes. And best of all, when she talked, when she offered a comment or insight, he seemed to take her seriously. He didn't talk down to her, and she didn't think she had to talk up to him.

"Don't let me bore you now, okay?" he said, calling her back from her reverie, shoving aside a stack of ungraded college-prep essays, showing his quick, confident smile. He was always fun to look at, thought Julie.

"Don't worry," she said. "If it drags, you'll get the Sign."

Conner bit his lip. "I'll chance it," he said.

"The Sign" was a little rolling gesture she made with her hand that told him to pick up the pace.

"Well," he began, taking a deep breath, leaning back in his swivel chair, "the Phantom came to Westpark one spring years ago, when the smoking problem outside the north end of the building had reached epidemic proportions. Of course our crack administration chose to look the other way. Any teachers stupid enough to intervene got stabbed in the back by Big D, who usually turned the offending student loose before the arresting teacher could even finish the disciplinary paperwork."

Julie gave him an amused look, shook her head, laughed.

"What is it?" asked Conner, grinning. "What's so funny? I haven't got to the good parts yet."

"You can't even mention Mr. Dolten without cutting him down," said Julie. "You're so judgmental sometimes."

"Let me put it this way," said Conner, an eyebrow arched. "When you see a man who's supposed to be your superior stand before a faculty meeting and snatch nose hairs for ten seconds, you might suspect he has one or two other social deficiencies."

Julie laughed again, her eyes squinting shut. Mr. Con-

2

ner's sarcasm always amused her, didn't threaten her. "Then what?" she said, catching her breath.

"Let's see. Some student reprisals went unpunished. One kid the German teacher nailed got even by spray painting the word NARK—that's N-A-R-K—on the side of Herr Steiner's brand-new car. Steiner laughed at the misspelling but not at the damage. So it was decided that somebody should take responsibility, somebody should circumvent the system and make things right."

"Were you the Phantom?"

"Yes and no," Conner answered with typical elusiveness, his bright gray eyes glittering. "Shall I try to continue? Or will it be useless?"

"It's your show."

So he recounted the Legend of the Phantom. He described how he and two social studies teachers had discovered a utility room with a metal staircase and a trapdoor leading to the roof. What the Phantom did was fill three large plastic wastebaskets with water, sneak them onto the roof, and wait until the smokers gathered below against the north wall. That area was seldom patrolled and completely screened from the view of any administrator's office. When the man responsible for spotting smokers swung by and tapped the go-ahead signal on the utility-room door, the other two hurried up the stairway, ran across the roof, and dumped the water onto the huddled masses below.

Julie chuckled as Mr. Conner described how the Nic-Nits looked and talked when they came stumbling back into the building, drenched.

"The what?" she asked.

"Nic-Nits. You know, Nicotine Nitwits."

"Of course."

"And because the Phantom struck at irregular inter-

3

vals, the smokers never got the jump on us. They became the Drowned Rat Regiment," said Mr. Conner.

"So where's the Phantom now?" asked Julie. "He hasn't been too active lately." She ran the side of her thumb down her cheek to get a strand of her thick brown hair away from her face.

"The Phantom's around. But he rarely shows himself."

"What happened to the Phantom Water-Dumper?" said Julie. "That's all I want to know."

"A couple of things brought the project to a sad end," Conner replied with mock seriousness. "For one, we underestimated the resourcefulness of the opposition, always a big mistake. During what turned out to be our second-to-the-last Phantom assault, our spotter noticed that three or four of the smokers had drifted away from the group and moved across the street. Before the spotter took off to give us the signal, he saw one of the drifters pull out a pair of binoculars while another aimed an expensive camera with a telephoto lens at the roof line. By acting quickly, our spotter was able to scrub the mission before we even opened the trapdoor."

"Close call."

"Very. But that's the one thing the Phantom always had going."

"What thing?"

"No one knew about the trapdoor or the stairway in the utility room. Those could be the only architectural secrets Dolten has managed to keep." Conner stopped again and slowly shook his head, his sinewy arms folded across his chest.

"Now what?" prompted Julie.

"The very last mission," he said. "I haven't thought about it for a long time."

4

"So tell me."

"We had a perfect plan," he said, winking. "We wanted to be on the roof early, before the photographer could set up. We intended to stay low, keep away from the camera. Even though we were up two and a half stories, we still had thirty hazardous feet to cover between the trapdoor and the roof edge. But we were ready to crawl the roof just to make the hit."

"Determination."

Conner nodded. "You bet. Anyway, on that particular morning, one of the last days of school, there were so many out puffing that the Phantom took it as a personal challenge."

"Not just a job but an adventure," teased Julie.

"Right. So there we were. I was up with my partner waiting for the spotter to join us. Usually we left the trapdoor open to make escaping easy and fast. But this time we closed it. Very early that morning it had rained, and it looked like it could start again any second."

"What'd you wear? Didn't you get dirty?"

"We had on some ratty sweat suits we borrowed from the phys ed equipment room. Along with work gloves and ski masks."

"Ski masks?" Julie said in amazement, fascinated by their daring, their guile. "And then?"

"We kept on waiting for the spotter to show. We'd hauled up two extra buckets, so we needed his help with the hit. We knew this was our last mission. We wanted perfection, a grand finale."

"I guess."

"So my partner and I waited and waited, belly-down on that filthy tar-and-gravel roof. We couldn't figure out what was keeping the spotter. Finally we crawled back to the trapdoor . . . and found it locked."

"Noooooo." Julie's eyes went wide.

"We pulled and twisted the handle, but we couldn't open it. Before we knew it, the bell rang. Now we were late, too. And there was no safe way down. Then, naturally, it started to rain. We didn't know whether to laugh or swear, so we did both. We stood there getting soaked, trying to figure some way out. Pretty soon the wind picked up and the rain started coming at us sideways."

Julie listened unblinking now, her lips slightly parted.

"Just when we were ready to try hanging over the edge and kicking in a window, the trapdoor opened. The spotter crawled out into the storm. He was woozy. He was holding his head with both hands. We ran for the trapdoor and scrambled down the stairs, pulling off the sweats and hiding them behind a transformer. As we rushed to our classes, we got the story."

"This is already a story!" Julie cut in. "Isn't it?"

"No. God's truth. It all happened."

"What happened?"

"Our spotter had gotten so excited that he'd raced up the stairs without noticing the trapdoor was closed. At full thrust, he slammed his head against the steel and knocked himself out. All he remembered was waking up on the floor with a bad head, neck, and back."

Once more Julie giggled.

"What's funny about that?" asked Conner, pretending to be insulted. "The man was a bona fide combat casualty."

"I don't believe this," said Julie.

"We're not done," replied Conner. "During class the next hour the storm really kicked up. Dolten panicked and called a tornado alert, so we had to herd all the kids into the basement. Down there, the Phantom met and talked over what had happened. After about five minutes of laughing and shushing each other, one of the others asked

6

me, 'You closed the door, right?' I stood there dazed for a three count. I couldn't for the life of me remember doing it. 'You did, didn't you?' the other guy said. When I told them I wasn't positive, the two of them said to watch their classes while they went back to check. Meanwhile the windows had started rattling so loudly we could hear it in the basement."

"Umm."

"I had to wait there another ten minutes before Dolten gave the all-clear announcement. My partners never came back down. I didn't see them again until I returned to the second floor myself. As I was walking past the men's room, they called to me from inside. The door was open a crack. I walked in and found them laughing so hard they could barely talk. Finally they explained how the wind had twisted the trapdoor nearly off its hinges. They had to force it shut. And by the time they did, so much water had poured in that the ceiling tiles in the utility room tore loose and the walls got soaked. They were in a very wet room with a million electrical wires—lotsa volts.

"After they'd hidden the ruined ceiling panels, they discovered how dirty they'd gotten. So they went to Dolten's office and told him they'd run outside during the storm, chasing three students trying to leave the building. 'No, Mr. Dolten, nosiree, we didn't catch 'em, uh-uh. Not this time. They got clean away.' " Conner gave Julie a quick nod and a tight-lipped smile.

"And that was the end of the Phantom?"

"The end of that project, yes."

"And no one ever found out about it—who did it, I mean?"

"The secret has been safe with me till now. I'd planned to carry it to the next world. But I've decided to trust you, and I think you know why."

7

"Why?"

"It's too soon to tell you that."

"Oh, nice. Fun and games now."

"Not at all. Never."

"Riiight," said Julie, getting up, knowing today's installment was over. She was already late for two meetings, one a student council committee discussion, the other a recruiting presentation by one of the eastern colleges she was applying to.

"So," continued Conner, "what did I learn from that experience? What did you learn from the Phantom?"

"It's too soon to tell," she replied, mimicking him. "I probably won't know what it means for a long time."

"That could be true. And that's a good attitude, the wait-and-see approach." He watched her closely as she gathered her books. "Have you done a serious job of revising your last essay?" he asked. "You know it's unthinkable to be doing so well on all the usage tests and performing below grade on the papers. Did you put some time and thought into this one? Did you decide to be yourself and deal with something you care about?"

"I'm working on it. Really," she said, noting his ironic look. "I've got to go now, okay?"

"Sure. I haven't bored you, have I? That's the one unforgivable sin in my credo—to bore another."

"If you bored me I'd tell you," she said with uncharacteristic boldness. Every time she made a comment like that she surprised herself. And she was making more and more of them whenever she talked with Mr. Conner. She was amazed she felt so at ease with him, especially considering that, though he'd been her college prep writing teacher for close to eight weeks, in many ways she barely knew him. But then again, she probably knew him better than any of the other students at Westpark.

"He's really different," said one of Julie's friends last year after finishing Conner's semester-long, seniors-only course.

"How do you mean?" Julie had asked.

"I can't say," the girl responded. "Mr. Conner can't be classified or summarized. He won't let you do that to him. He'll play a certain part for a day or a week, and just when you think you have him figured out, he'll change. He can't be described. He must simply be experienced. If he worked anywhere but here, they'd probably commit him to a mental ward. He's unstable, but he's also quite creative, I think. Maybe brilliant. Just remember when you're in there not to believe everything you see."

And that was all Julie could get from anybody who'd taken Mr. Conner's course. It was as though, like some Cosa Nostra don, he had pledged his former students to the Rule of Silence. So Julie was more than a little surprised to find herself his confidante.

When she started to leave, he got up and opened the door for her.

"See ya," she said, wondering where it would all lead.

"Oh, you've seen me already, and I'm sure you'll see a lot more," he commented.

She headed down the empty corridor, thinking it was a wonderful feeling to be trusted, to find someone she could trust. But before Julie had taken five strides, Mr. Conner called her back.

"What is it?" she asked as she stepped into his room again. He eased the door shut and stood very close to her, looking warmly down at her upturned, flawless face.

"Guess," he said softly.

Julie took a deep breath, felt vaguely threatened for a moment. "I can't guess," she answered quietly.

"I do believe you're the one, Juliet."

"The one what?" she said, backing away a half step.

"The very one who can do it."

"Do *what?*" she asked, hoping for a quick end to this silly cat-and-mouse routine.

"How would you, Juliet Lamar, like to play the lead in . . . a psychodrama?"

"What's a psychodrama?"

"I can't tell you right now," he said.

"Not that line again," said Julie.

Conner laughed softly. "Look, just think about it while I work out the details. For our purposes, it will be a sort of . . . morality play, a kind of theatrical Phantomizing, high art. Trust me, okay?"

Julie looked skeptically at him. She knew he was being mildly ironic with her now. Even a little patronizing. She shook her head. "I don't know about you, Mr. Conner."

"That's just as well at this point. But please consider taking the role, okay? And of course don't mention any of this to anybody."

Julie looked away. "You didn't have to tell me that. I can keep my mouth shut. I know how it is with you."

"I shouldn't have said anything. I'm sorry."

"That's okay. Will you promise to tell me more soon, or is this a long-range project?"

"As soon as I can, and that'll be very soon."

Conner continued to smile, but Julie noticed his eyes were intent: he was somehow still measuring or judging her.

"What now?" she asked to break the awkward silence.

"I envy you."

"Why?"

"Because you're at a wonderful time in your life, and you have what really matters."

"Yeah? And what's that?" asked Julie, suspicious again.

"You have the intelligence, energy, and beauty to control your destiny. You have the power to define yourself any way you want to."

They looked into each other's eyes for a long moment.

"Thanks for coming back," Conner said, ending the conversation.

"Bye again," said Julie, opening the door.

"See ya soon," replied Conner, pointing his right index finger at her like the barrel of a gun.

CHAPTER 2

That evening while Julie tried to do her physics and calculus and college prep writing homework, all she could think about was Mr. Conner. She'd been working at her desk for less than an hour when she abruptly stopped doing math and reached for her Westpark Warrior yearbook. She wanted to look up Mr. Conner's faculty picture. In it he was dressed as a French chef, complete with a puffy white barrel hat and a waxed and curled fake mustache. Behind him on the blackboard he had written: "Good ingredients precede good writing."

She laughed out loud. She had looked through this yearbook dozens of times since getting it last spring, but she'd never thought that picture unusual. Now she knew better. She recalled the first day of Mr. Conner's class this year . . . and smiled.

Typically, on opening day at Westpark, most of the

male faculty members showed up for work looking more like the custodians of the cafeteria than the custodians of culture. Their cheap, stained and faded golf shirts, ill-fitting off-brand blue jeans, and tattered running shoes testified to their reluctance to end another summer and start another school year.

Mr. Conner, on the other hand, had swept into his classroom wearing a flawless cream-colored three-piece tropical-weight suit, a light-blue Oxford shirt, a subtly patterned navy tie, and a white wide-brimmed planter's hat. Julie didn't know if his outfit was a joke or a gesture of respect for his students and his work.

"So tell me somethin' now, mah s'posedly emancipated colleagues," he began with a heavy southern accent. Then, his brows knit, he asked, "Are y'all *slaves* to *clichés?* Are y'all *repressed* by the *ready-made?* Are y'all really *free* to *see* and *be?*" He stared wide-eyed at them, seeming to encourage a response, but somehow letting them know that he expected nothing. The class gave him what he expected. Julie had sneaked a look at the other members of the group, all of whom sat slack-jawed with confusion.

"Well, m'friends, let me say that liberation looms on your horizon." And with that pronouncement he removed his hat in a sweeping stroke and bowed. That's how he had introduced himself on the first day of class early last September.

Mr. Conner continued the introductory lecture by claiming that people could be slaves to language and thus slaves to the people who enslave with language. "Or," he had said, "you can set yourself free by being the master of your language instead of its victim." He'd concluded by promising, "If you work hard this semester, you will win your freedom."

Then suddenly he changed, became another character—a drill sergeant or something. He dropped the planter's hat on his desk and glowered at them. "Welcome to college prep writing, section three," he said gruffly, sarcastically, his back straight, his chin tucked.

Alert, anxious Juliet Lamar, sitting halfway down the first row, watched her teacher as he read the class list clutched in his right hand while slowly raising his left arm, pointing his middle three fingers at them.

When he'd finished taking roll, he boomed, "We are here officially to learn one thing!" Now he waggled his left index finger. "And that's how to write those cursed freshman comp essays! Ours will be a back-to-basics, boot camp approach to composition. If you like diligence, discipline, and a little degradation, you'll like this course. If you don't like those things, you'll learn to like them better . . . or else."

Julie smiled and Conner caught her at it. For a split second he stared at her with a knowing intensity that made her feel uneasy. She averted her eyes, confused. Hadn't he just contradicted himself? What did he want them to be? Foot soldiers? Freedom fighters? Both?

Glancing again at the yearbook, Julie remembered how much she'd enjoyed watching Mr. Conner that first day, looking at his long, dark, perfectly-styled wavy hair, his smooth, tanned, clean-shaven boyish face, the animal grace of his movements, the controlled expressiveness of even his smallest gesture. His smile was especially attractive. It was warm, bright, and vaguely enigmatic.

After a month of class, Julie decided Mr. Conner's opening-day wardrobe had definitely been a costume. Since then he'd posed as many different characters, each one reinforcing some point he was trying to make about their writing. He was actually obsessive about role-playing.

For instance, once he came dressed as a policeman to

point out that they must "arrest and eradicate whatever was flip, glib, and fake" in their papers. A week later he appeared in work boots, blue jeans, a T-shirt, and a hard hat to assert that "good writing is architecture, not interior decoration." Another day he impersonated a stereotypical old-time movie director, clad in a yellow silk shirt, pleated white wool pants, white buck shoes, and a black beret. In his right hand he carried a small megaphone; in his left, a riding crop. He snapped the riding crop down hard on his desk each time he made a point.

With a heavy lisp, he proclaimed, "You, my dears, simply must focus on specifics! You must startle with scenes that stimulate! In short, you must eschew the sweeping overview! *Eschew the sweeping overview!*" he cried conclusively, clasping his hands together under his chin.

Then, cracking the riding crop to accent every word, he yelled, "In your essays, let me *see somebody doing something!*" With that he bowed and swept out of the room, striding smartly.

"Whadda jerk," mumbled Kevin Ellison, who sat across the aisle from Julie. He was talking to no one in particular. Julie knew Kevin found Conner's performances eyeglazing.

On two other occasions Mr. Conner had come in costume. Once, as a pirate, he talked on the theme "A good writer doesn't borrow, he steals." He'd explained that maxim by saying, "Each of you can and must take possession of experience by shaping it in thought." And most recently he appeared as a rumpled cockney gravedigger who spoke on the topic of "Composition and Decomposition, or What Do You Do When You Think You're Done?"

Although Julie had enjoyed the costume shows immensely, she wasn't sure yet if they'd been understood or appreciated by most of the students. Julie recalled some of the other strange things he'd done during the first few weeks of class. One day he charged into the room with a set of themes that he threw down on his desk so hard the noise startled and silenced the group.

He hollered, "Don't you people know *anything* about organization? Didn't you ever have to *plan* anything beforehand? With very few exceptions, these were the most poorly organized essays I've ever read. So it's become obvious to me that we can't simply talk about organization, we've got to *live it*!

"From now on then, for the sake of developing an attitude of respect for organization, I want you to consider the first person in each row as the row captain. The row captain is responsible for the performance of each member of his or her row. The row captain is answerable to me, for I'm the *capo di tutti capi*—loosely translated, the captain of all captains. Furthermore, it's the row captain's job to keep everyone together."

Then, addressing the row captains specifically, Conner continued, "My captains, you must never ever leave casualties on the battlefield. You must see that the members of your row learn how to help each other whenever it's appropriate. And you will never consider retreat. Pursue the assignments relentlessly. Never surrender. Don't ever give up on an assignment and say it can't be done." He sized up his row captains then with a severe glance.

"By the end of the hour today," he added, "I want all of you to meet first with your row captain and then as a class. You must decide a few things. Before you leave, I want to know your class name or mascot, one that embodies the attitude we're trying to establish; your class colors; your class motto. These are important decisions and shouldn't be taken lightly. Your choices will determine the tone of your experience in here, the character of this group."

Ominously, by majority vote, Julie's third-hour section adopted the colors black and blue, the team name Troy's Toys, and the team motto "Things are never so bad they can't be worse."

But at the end of the week, in apparent contradiction to what he'd been preaching since Monday, Mr. Conner announced, "You should know, of course, that a beautifully organized essay, like a beautifully organized life, is nothing in comparison to a beautifully expressive one. An essay, after all, is not a mine field where you're struggling merely to survive, to avoid some fatal mistake. It's an open-ended opportunity to explore freely."

Julie turned pages in her yearbook, leaving the picture of Mr. Conner as a French chef and looking for some of herself. She'd had a wonderful junior year. That was the only way to describe it. She'd done it all last year, and this yearbook was her record of it, her evidence that it had all really happened. It told her again and again who she was last year, what she had achieved.

Last fall she'd been voted a member of the homecoming court. During the winter she was a basketball cheerleader for a championship team. By June she had not only lettered in track but also performed in the spring play. She had tried to take on every possible challenge last year, win respect, *be somebody*, just as her father commanded.

Throughout most of that year she had dated one boy, a senior named Brad Bennett. She had gotten to know him while serving on the student council. Brad had been perfect for her last year—calming and polite and considerate and sensitive and sincere and not at all jealous of her success. He was a nice guy.

But by spring they both realized it was over. Julie no longer needed Brad's steadying influence. She was ready to move on. And so was he. She knew he was going far away to attend college, and that the security of having a

17

girl back home was usually a quickly discarded crutch. So they split, amicably but irrevocably.

A week after Brad graduated, his family moved to Dallas, Texas. So he burned his bridges, including the one to Julie. He hadn't written to her once since moving and starting school at Texas Tech, where he studied electrical engineering. The smoke cleared quickly and painlessly, though. Now only good memories of Brad remained.

All those things had happened last year. As Julie closed the book, she felt that if her experiences hadn't been so thoroughly documented, she might doubt they'd actually happened. It already seemed so long ago. She sighed, amazed at how far she'd come since arriving in Minneapolis the year before last. She still remembered vividly the agonizing loneliness she'd felt as a new student at Westpark. She had been hurting back then.

The summer before her sophomore year her parents had divorced. Before that, the three of them had been living in a beautiful suburb north of Chicago. Her father was an aggressive and successful advertising executive, her mother a legal researcher. After the divorce, her dad returned to his hometown of Boston while her mother sought refuge with friends in Minneapolis. The two of them, mother and daughter, had lived quietly in a spacious suburban apartment complex for over two years now.

Throughout her sophomore year Julie had tried to stay close to her father by writing to him every week and calling him twice a month. At first he responded to all her letters, but soon his replies became brief and infrequent. She'd visited him during their first summer apart and found him living with another woman. It quickly became obvious to Julie that he hadn't thought much about who his daughter was becoming or how she fit into his new life. It was an awkward two-week stay.

During her junior year, he had written enthusiastic congratulatory notes every time she sent him an article about one of her successes, but when summer came, there was no invitation to visit Boston. For six months Julie had heard nothing at all from her father.

Fortunately, the anger and frustration resulting from her father's betrayal and rejection hadn't been more than Julie could handle. She'd suffered, but survived. She had sought refuge, acceptance, and security at school. And she'd won it, won it in a big way. But she continued to hope for the moment when she'd won enough to earn her dad's approval again, to win him back.

Recently she'd found comfort in her art, her painting, though that source of solace was also becoming unreliable. In the past, whenever the pressure of *everything* became too much, Julie would retreat to her room for entire weekends and lose herself in a painting. But the last two times, getting lost had left her terrified rather than tranquilized.

The paintings that evolved from those sessions were collagelike explorations haunted by images of her father, his face. Each time Julie tried to capture his features, she found herself being drawn more and more into the drama on the canvas, the conflict there an echo of the struggle in her heart. She noticed that none of the images resembled any other and congratulated herself on catching his many moods. When she finally grasped the real reason for the uncertainty of her images—that she no longer knew exactly what he looked like or who he was—she destroyed the canvases and quit, frightened. The art game was over.

But now, just at the right time, she'd found a new game, a more promising game. It involved Mr. Conner . . . and the future.

With her father out East, she wanted more than anything to attend college there. He'd always told her, "Don't ever go second class, sweetheart. Take yourself seriously and take yourself as far as you can go. That's the only way you'll get there. Remember, it's not just 'Be all that you can be.' The thing is to be *more* than you can be, more than you're supposed to be." Maybe she was still her father's daughter after all.

So this year her needs, her goals, had changed dramatically. For Juliet Lamar, high school was over. Westpark social life was not the solution anymore. She was growing up, and she knew it. It was now time to plan for college.

When she told her mother about her desire to go east and study English and Spanish and French and art and theater and whatever else it would take for her to get a teaching job in an American school in Europe, her mother was supportive. "Be independent," her mother had said. "Be strong. See the world. Live your own dreams."

Julie listened.

"You know me," her mother continued. "I love to hide, in a book or in my work. But you're not like me."

"Sure I am."

"Maybe sometimes. But it's not a good way to be. The older I get, the fewer risks I want to take. That's sad, and limiting. I don't want you to miss your chance."

"I know," said Julie. "I won't miss it. I just can't."

So now Julie was in the process of applying to Bennington, Bryn Mawr, Radcliffe, and Wellesley, and it was for that reason, to get help with the essays required for her applications, that she'd decided after only six weeks of class to make an appointment with Mr. Conner.

She had felt optimistic about seeing him because he had liked her writing. She had been receiving more positive than negative comments on her essays, a phenomenon that put her in the upper 10 percent of her class. Most of the students were struggling horribly to say anything that wasn't plagued by "derivative abstractions, oversimplified pronouncements, smug generalizations, and assembly-line language."

In keeping with his boot-camp approach to composition, Conner made them feel worthless until they met his standards, learned what he wanted them to know, and did what he wanted them to do. He wanted to see who among them "could take it." He wanted to instill in them a lasting aversion to sloppiness and a hunger for precision.

Unlike her classmates, Julie was receiving comments such as "I admire your awareness of the complexity of this issue. Good work." That was Conner's response to her "definition of an abstract term" essay. She had written on trust, arguing that honesty and trust were the most important parts of true friendship. Best of all, she had loaded the paper with vivid specific examples from her own painful recent experience that "convincingly illustrated" her thesis. So, feeling confident, she requested a meeting after school.

Thinking about those applications brought Julie again to the present. She put the yearbook back on the shelf and picked up the manila folder containing copies of her essays.

When she'd first asked Conner for help, he had asked, "What's your philosophy of life?"

She'd looked at him quizzically and shrugged.

"You must develop a philosophically consistent persona in essays like these, because if they're good, if the person the reviewer meets in them is attractive and interesting, an interview with someone from the school will follow. Big-league schools are looking for big-league people, so you'll want to be the same person *in person* that you appear to be on paper. Okay?"

"I understand," Julie said.

21

Conner stood up and closed the door to his room, shutting out the hallway noise. "So what's your philosophy?"

"I'm not sure," Julie answered with a thin, embarrassed smile.

"Not sure?" Conner replied sarcastically, placing his palm on his chest, a gesture of exaggerated surprise and astonishment. "Did you really say *not sure*?"

"I'm afraid so." Julie looked down at her hands, which were folded in her lap.

"Would you like to find out?"

"You can tell me what my philosophy of life is?"

"I can give you a chance to discover it for yourself," Conner answered. "That's the best thing any teacher can do for a student, right?"

"Right."

"You see, I've got this little test," he continued in a near whisper, leaning closer to Julie, giving her a heart-melting conspiratorial wink. "Interested?"

Julie shrugged, smiled innocently. She looked at him and felt a faint tightness at the back of her throat.

"Wouldn't you like to find out if you're an idealist, a realist, a pragmatist, or a flaming existentialist?"

"Oh, sure," Julie answered. "Absolutely."

So she took Mr. Conner's test, a collection of a hundred statements about reality and morality and values and perception. When she had finished rating the statements as agreeable or disagreeable to her, Conner evaluated her responses and pronounced her a "pragmatist with strong existentialistic tendencies."

"What does that mean?" she asked.

"You're creative and flexible and adaptable. Change and challenge don't frighten you. You not only accept them as inevitable but look forward to them as opportunities. Basically you're a seeker. Am I right? Is that you?"

"Sometimes, I guess. What are you?" she asked quickly, challenging Conner.

"Oh, the same, the same," he said.

"You're teasing."

"No, I'm not. Not at all. That's my outlook, too." He gave her an earnest stare, but something in his eyes told her his pose was ironic. "And from now on, after you write these application statements, it had better be your outlook *consistently*. And I mean all the time. One other thing . . ." He paused, waiting for her to respond.

"What?" Their eyes met, held. "What?" she repeated.

"Don't ever, whatever you do, get seriously involved with a humorless engineer or a fundamentalist preacher."

"Why?"

"Trust me," Conner had said. "It would end in a philosophical Battle Grand that would leave you wasted, or at least severely wounded. Maybe even profoundly jaded."

"Really?"

"Uh-huh. Would I lie? You do trust me?"

"Can I wait to answer that?" she responded, even though she knew a bond was forming between them.

The first thing Julie did after the meeting was go to the library and check out several books on contemporary philosophy. After scanning a few chapters in each, she still had only some vague notions about what pragmatism and existentialism were. Still, she wrote her application essays, and after reading them, Mr. Conner had said, "Yes, these are fine. I can admire them, and so will many others."

The day Mr. Conner returned the drafts to Julie, he'd pulled them from his ever-present black briefcase. While the case sat open, Julie had noticed two things. One was a worn 5×7 black-and-white photograph taped neatly to an inside panel. It was a picture of two soldiers, both wearing steel helmets and camouflage fatigues and flak jackets, both with bandoliers of ammunition draped over

23

their shoulders and crossing their chests Mexican-bandit style. Behind them was a waist-high wall of sandbags.

"Are you one of those guys?" Julie asked curiously.

"What?" Mr. Conner said as he followed her line of vision to the picture. For once he seemed startled. "Oh, that. Yes, I'm the one on the left."

"Really? It doesn't look like you at all."

"I was a different person then. I was a lot younger."

"How old were you?"

"Nineteen, almost twenty."

"Who's the other guy?"

"A friend."

"Where are you? Vietnam?"

"You got it. That's beautiful Phu Bai in the background," said Conner, looking at her essays now and not at the photograph—trying, Julie imagined, to seem indifferent. "Some journalist took it and sent me a copy."

"Oh," said Julie as if that cleared everything up.

"Aren't you wondering why I keep it there?" asked Mr. Conner, facing Julie again, staring unblinking into her dark brown eyes.

"I guess."

He thought a moment before answering. "It helps me remember who I am, and how it is."

"I don't understand."

"You will," said Conner, easing the briefcase shut.

"Can I ask another personal question?"

"How personal?"

"Your initials," she said, pointing at the briefcase, at the gold letters T.M.C. embossed near the handle. "What does the M stand for?"

He let a moment pass, then said, "You won't laugh?"

"Uh-uh."

"Merlin."

24

"No."

"Yeah."

"The magician," she said thoughtfully.

"Sure."

"But he wasn't real."

"He wasn't?"

"He wasn't a real person. That's what Mr. Oakley said in mythology last year."

"That Merlin never lived?"

"Right, he never lived."

Conner leaned close again and said, "Of course he does."

Julie sat at her bedroom desk now and closed the manila folder on her essays. She thought about the past and the future. The immediate past had been pleasant but somehow unsatisfying. The distant future seemed strangely unfocused, dim, and even a little intimidating despite her efforts to plan for it. The immediate future, though, seemed bright. Mr. Conner had asked to see her after school . . . again.

She realized he was quickly becoming the great thing she'd lost when her parents broke up—someone who paid attention.

CHAPTER
3

M r. Conner said, "I have another story." He eased the door shut and followed Julie over to his desk. As usual, she sat down in the guest chair, a molded-plastic-and-aluminum marvel.

"Okay," said Julie. "Shoot."

Conner chuckled.

"What's so funny?"

"You'll see." Sitting down himself, leaning back and lacing his hands behind his head, Conner asked, "Do you remember a teacher named Bruce Beekman, a little balding guy with glasses who taught speech and always wore banker's suits?"

"He was here when I was a sophomore, I think."

"Right. That was his last year with us, his final campaign."

"Why?"

"Why what?"

"Why was it his final campaign?"

"He'd had it. He couldn't take any more abuse from the basic comp bozos. And from other people on the staff who misunderstood him. They thought he was arrogant, pompous, and self-serving because he tried to have his debate program labeled a 'varsity sport,' complete with letter sweaters and pep assemblies." Conner nodded absently, remembering. Julie waited and watched as a small, knowing grin formed. "You recall him, then?" Conner asked.

"I guess."

"And do you know Mr. Tom Prentiss in social studies?"

"Do I ever. I had him for World History I *and* II!"

"So you may be aware that he is somewhat . . . bombastic? Yes?"

"Yes."

"And opinionated?"

"Uh-huh."

"Even bellicose?"

"That too."

"Intimidating? Insulting? Insensitive?"

"Yes, yes," said Julie, brightening. "All those!"

"Well, a couple of years before you came to Westpark, we had . . ."—Conner paused, let the drama build—"an incident. Throughout that year and the three before it, Prentiss had made Beekman his whipping boy, his verbal punching bag. On bad days Beekman merely had to enter the English / social studies office and Prentiss was all over him like, like—"

"Bees on honey?" Julie ventured.

"That's acceptable, thanks," said Conner, rolling his eyes. "Like bees on honey. Anyway, Prentiss began razzing Beekman every single day. It was always 'friendly teasing,' but endless friendly teasing can have a very negative cumulative effect, you know?"

"I know."

27

"Eventually Beekman got tired of having his clothes, physique, teaching skill, car, house, and even his wife maligned. So one day Bruce came to me for help. And we formulated a plan, a script. And we set the stage." Conner stared directly at Julie and said, "Are you with me on this? Still listening?"

"Sure."

"Not bored?"

"C'mon, keep going," she said, slapping at Conner.

"That's excessive force, miss," Conner replied, pretending to shield himself.

"I'm ready," she said, waving a small fist at him, "to *make* you talk."

"My threshold of pain is scandalously low," Conner said. "I'll spill. Just don't hit me."

"That's more like it. Go on."

"What happened was this. We planned to catch Prentiss right after school. He always came into the office then. He'd sit down in his chair, put his feet up on his desk, and read the paper until quitting time. The day we chose to do it, Prentiss was all alone in the office."

"Who's we?"

"Beekman, MacDonald, and me."

"Mr. MacDonald was in on it?" said Julie, surprised. "He seems too old and too dignified for your kind of—"

"Entertainment?"

"Mischief."

"But that's why he was perfect for the part."

"Then what?"

"Predictably, as soon as Beekman came strolling into the office Prentiss attacked. That day Beekman wore his blue-striped seersucker suit, an outfit Prentiss found particularly threatening and offensive. Don't ask me why. 'My god, Brucie!' said Prentiss. 'Will you lay that loony-tune getup to rest? Those went out after World War Two!'

28

"Just then MacDonald and I entered the office. Leaning further back in his chair, Prentiss said to us, 'Willya look at him? *Geek*man's got his snoot suit out of mothballs again!' Prentiss had barely finished when Beekman said, 'Prentiss, I've had it with you. I'm not taking your mindless contumely anymore.'

" 'Oh, really?' said Prentiss, cocking an eyebrow, ready for a confrontation. But before he could launch another gibe, Beekman pulled a nickel-plated starter's pistol from his suit jacket and aimed it across the room at Prentiss. Just as Prentiss's eyes popped with awareness and real fear, MacDonald stepped into the line of fire and waved his hands at Beekman, pleading with him not to shoot. But he was too late. Beekman pulled the trigger."

"What? He shot him?"

"Beekman squeezed off one deafening round. Of course the gun was filled with .22 blanks, but the noise took Prentiss's breath away. In the split second after the explosion, I yelled, 'No, Bruce!' while MacDonald, who was still facing Beekman, groaned loudly, clutched his chest, and stumbled back into Prentiss, landing heavily in his lap, knocking him off the chair onto the floor.

"With MacDonald's 'corpse' still on top of him, Prentiss started screaming 'AH-YEE! AH-YEE! AH-YEE!' as he tried to catch his breath and get out from under. Pretty soon other teachers and some students came in from the hall, gaping as Bruce and I stood around chanting 'AH-YEE!' in time with Prentiss. Then MacDonald really broke up. Most fun he'd ever had, I guess.

"The second Prentiss understood what was going on, he heaved MacDonald away and tried to stand, wanted to hit somebody. But his legs were rubber. His face was red, and he still couldn't get a full breath. He collapsed as he threw a careless punch Beekman's way.

"Beekman smiled at him, blew imaginary smoke from

29

the barrel of his gun, and started to walk out. Then Prentiss croaked, 'S'not over yet, you creep!' Beekman ignored him. 'S'not over yet!' Prentiss yelled again. But Tom never taunted Beekman after that." Conner smiled at Julie. "Good story, huh?"

Julie, astonished, mesmerized, was unable to comment.

"You liked it?" asked Conner. "Did you?"

She nodded. "Yes," she said finally. "But why do you tell me this stuff?"

"Someone should know. It's particularly important now to share our rich anecdotal heritage here at Westpark, the myths and legends. It's a body of knowledge that must live on." Conner narrowed his eyes, glanced to either side, then looked straight at her. "Would you like to do something like that?" he asked.

"Huh? Like what?" She was suddenly serious, wary.

"Would you like to try that routine?"

"You mean shoot somebody?"

"In a manner of speaking, yes."

"Who?"

"Why, me, of course," Conner answered.

"Wait a minute," said Julie suspiciously. "Are we talking psychodrama now?"

"Could be," Conner replied.

"What is it *exactly*?"

"It's lots of things. It's a wonderful mixing of art and life, all done for the higher purpose of discovering truth. If the other students get caught up in the action rather than waiting passively for an explanation, they'll have a chance to learn something about themselves. You still with me?"

"Uh-huh."

"So we stage a scene, an authentic-looking confrontation. Then we watch and measure and evaluate their

30

reactions. We'll see people struggle to understand a situation that doesn't make sense in light of what they think they know."

"What kind of scene?" asked Julie, more curious now than ever, more aware than ever that she was about to cross an important boundary. Where she was heading was a complete but intriguing mystery.

"Here's what I had in mind,"said Conner. "Tell me if you're comfortable with it." Then Conner explained how during the next week they would manufacture a "precipitating incident."

"Like what?" Julie asked.

Conner summarized the detailed plot he'd already worked out.

Julie liked the idea of taking a dare, of stepping outside the routine, the increasing tedium of her world. When she consented to play a part in the psychodrama, Conner said, "You sure you understand completely what you're getting into, the risk involved?"

"Why ask that? What else should I know?"

"One, that being part of this will change things forever for both of us. You'll be remembered as the one who did it, and I as the one who caused it. You'll be a credit to your class, and I'll be the creep. Second, this whole thing could explode in our faces. It could really cost us."

"How?"

"If anyone ever thought we staged this purely for our own amusement, purely to put one over on the rest of the class, we could both be ostracized for real. Understand now?"

"Don't tell anybody. That's the gist, right?"

"The ultimate gist, yes. And remember, if this thing works, you'll be in a dream situation. You'll be able to find out, for better or worse, what other people really think of you. As for our audience, they'll have the chance to make some decisions on important issues and learn more about themselves. See? There's something in this for everybody. We're after genuine heartfelt responses from your classmates. We want to see their feelings plainly, and stated forcefully, no matter what those feelings are, okay? So knowing all that, you still want to do it?"

"Sure," Julie answered quietly, looking at the floor, then glancing up and meeting Conner's eyes. "I need some excitement about now."

He smiled quizzically and then added, "Me too. You can handle the pressure?"

"I hope so."

"All right then," said Conner, sitting forward, placing his forearms on his thighs. "We probably shouldn't meet again until after D day, so if you have any more questions, you'd better ask them now. Are you entirely comfortable with the plan?"

"You've got it all figured out."

"But are you happy with it? This is your last chance to revise the script. After today, events will take on a life of their own."

"I understand," said Julie. "I like it the way it is."

"I'm glad." He smiled warmly, then asked, "Want to take a second and practice your crucial shot?"

"Absolutely."

So they rehearsed a few times, had some laughs.

Conner ended it with, "I knew after just one conversation that you were right for this project."

"Why do you keep saying that?"

"Because from what I can tell, from what you've said, from what I've seen, you're *in* this school in every obvious way you can be, but you're not really *of* it anymore. Right? You see this place for what it is. You're at a crossroads. You're ready for a change."

Julie shrugged.

"You're a very private person," Conner teased, a lop-sided grin inviting Julie to comment.

"I am, yes. And I'm all those other things, too. How'd you know all that?"

"The great director sees all and knows all," replied Conner in a low voice.

"What else do you know about me?"

"Well, you seem to be friendly with people from lots of different groups, but nobody really knows you."

Julie nodded again, wrinkles of amazement lining her forehead.

"You're respected and admired, Julie, but just aloof enough to be mysterious. You're the archetypal *unknown quantity*. You're perfect for the part."

"You really think so?"

"I do." He paused a moment before extending his hand. "Good luck, comrade," he said. "Our mission is fraught with peril, but it could also bring both of us great rewards."

Julie reached out and took his hand and sealed the bargain, feeling deeply excited by the prospect of the psychodrama. She felt a soothing, gentle pressure from Mr. Conner's hand before she released it. She stood up to leave.

"Do you realize, Juliet, that if all goes well, a good ninety percent of the stuff people write in your yearbook will be about this? You're betting the house."

"No lie."

"Would I lie?" asked Conner.

"I hope not. Would you?"

"C'mon."

"Well . . . bye," said Julie.

"Be ready for anything," Conner advised.

Julie had just left Mr. Conner's room when she ran into high-strung Shauna Saunders in the hall. As always, Shauna was with her boyfriend, Mike Bryant, super-jock. Julie had been on the cheerleading squad with Shauna last winter and had developed the kind of faky familiarity typical of that Westpark crowd.

"My, my, *my*," said Shauna softly, touching Julie's forearm, but looking past her toward Mr. Conner's door. "What have we here?" she continued. "In seeing him *again*, Julie?" Shauna's smile went off and on like a failing fluorescent bulb.

"What's that supposed to mean?" asked Julie, feigning amused naïveté.

"What is it now, Mike?" said Shauna, looking at her "big blond buckeroo," as she called him. "Four times in the last two weeks?"

Mike Bryant, to his credit, shrugged and looked away. Either he's blind to what Shauna's suggesting, thought Julie, or he's as bored as I am by this conversation.

"Four times what?" asked Julie, maintaining her pose.

"I admit, woman, he's awfully pretty. And a good grade from him means something. But isn't it a little dangerous to play *that* game? I mean, everyone knows Mr. Conner's reputa—"

"Shauna dear," Julie interrupted, "I hate to disappoint you, but he's only helping me with some essays for college applications. Want to see the rough drafts?" Julie hoped Shauna wouldn't call her bluff.

"No need to, dear. No need to. I understand," said Shauna with an exaggerated wink. "Just remember, Julie, not everyone's as blind as you think. Some things are pretty obvious and not very healthy, if you get my meaning."

"I'll remember you said that," replied Julie, donning her best bogus smile, yet another by-product of her cheerleading experience.

"Just trying to be a friend," Shauna said. Then she

34

shook back her long, curly bleached-blond hair and saun-
tered off with Mike, whispering and giggling.

Julie turned and hurried toward her locker.

While she walked home, Julie kept thinking that despite
their alleged closeness, she didn't actually know the first
thing about Mr. Conner. Where did he live? Was he mar-
ried? A father? Did he have brothers and sisters? Where
had he gone to college? What did he do during the sum-
mers? She knew nothing.

By the time she reached home she had realized that
all she knew about him was what he'd told her, what he'd
allowed her to know. Beginning to panic, she decided it
might be a good idea to find out whether Mr. Conner had
ever tried this kind of thing before with other students.
But she couldn't think of a way to ask around without
incriminating herself, without revealing complicity in her
own psychodrama. She made a mental note to find out as
much as she could about him anyway. Soon she was feeling
downright treacherous. But she wasn't sure whom she was
deceiving. Her classmates? Her teacher? Herself?

I'm in over my head, she concluded as she entered the
apartment.

CHAPTER
4

When Juliet Lamar walked into Troy Conner's college prep writing class the next day, she was a girl plagued by doubt. Her insecurity followed from the wasted detective work she'd done last night and that morning. At home she had tried looking up Mr. Conner's number in the thick municipal directory. She assumed he would be listed there because supposedly he lived "way out by a lake someplace" on the far west side of the city. That was the generally accepted belief among Mr. Conner's students, though no one claimed to know exactly which lake. Not finding his name in the phone book, Julie called information. The operator told her, "That number is unlisted. Sorry."

"So am I," Julie said to herself after she'd hung up.

Before school she'd tried yet another tack. She had gone into the crowded attendance office, worked her way to the student emergency phone at the end of the long white Formica counter, and sneaked a look at the district staff directory, which was under a stack of three or four other city and suburban phone books. In it she found only Conner's name and subject area, no address or phone number. A quick thumbing through the booklet revealed that all the other faculty members had provided the information. Julie knew then that only Conner could tell her why he hadn't. So she drifted toward his third-hour class still haunted by uncertainty.

Once there, she didn't have long to contemplate her predicament. Almost immediately after the bell stopped ringing, Mr. Conner rushed in and said, "Okay, no delay, get out the work that's due today!"

The homework assignment had been to complete a work sheet, a "grammar/usage review opportunity," in Mr. Conner's terms. For this particular exercise they had to label twenty sentences according to the kinds of clauses contained in them. Typically, Julie was one of the few who had finished the assignment and come to class prepared to discuss it. She was often mystified by students who refused to prepare for Conner's class despite the verbal abuse they received if they were found out. Such demeaning assaults were Conner's way of dealing with "laggards." His approach to grammar and usage, he said, was premised on the wisdom of Ben Franklin: "Those things that hurt, instruct." So he attempted to "teach by trauma," and when he chanced upon an ill-prepared student, considering all the warnings he had issued, it irritated him to no end.

"All right!" he yelled. "Get 'em out!"

Julie's classmates made a big show of rattling their homework sheets down on their desktops. Conner wasted no time. He went right after slouching Kevin Ellison. But surprisingly, miraculously, Kevin correctly answered each of Conner's questions.

Before Julie could draw another breath, Conner called

on her. "Miss Lamar," he said unctuously, shooting her a sharp glance full of challenge.

"Yes?"

"Tell me all about sentence number twelve, will you? Read it out loud first."

So Julie read, " 'I waited until after supper; then I told my mother the news.' "

"Very good," remarked Conner as he paced slowly back and forth in front of them. "Now what is the first clause you see?"

" 'I waited.' "

"Yes. And the next?"

" 'I told.' "

"That's true. That's very true. And how are they joined?"

"With a semicolon."

"Which makes both clauses . . . "

"Independent," said Julie.

"So we have what kind of a sentence structurally?"

"Compound."

"Very, very good, Miss Lamar. Now," he said ominously, "let's get serious. Let's take a much closer look at this sentence, okay? Let's consider the sociopsychological implications."

Julie felt a white-hot wave of panic roll through her body. She had said everything she was prepared to say about this sentence. She had no idea what Conner was going to ask next or where he was planning to take her.

"Okay," she answered, her voice hesitant.

"Okay," he repeated, donning a malicious smile. "What about 'the news' Miss Lamar?" he asked.

"Pardon?"

" 'The news.' In the sentence you just read. What about it?"

"What do you mean, what about it?" Julie answered, an edge of irritation in her voice.

"In that sentence, Miss Lamar, you mentioned 'the news.' "

"Uh-huh."

"What about it?"

"The news?"

"*Yes*," he snapped.

By now laughter was bubbling up from the edges of the classroom. Julie felt her face grow hot, a blush of embarrassment running up her throat and exploding in her cheeks. "I don't understand what you want," she said at last.

"What I want is what you want, Miss Lamar. What everyone in the class wants right now," Conner answered, ridiculing her with his tone. "I want to know what kind of news someone would wait until *after* supper to tell his or her mother."

The class roared. Even Julie laughed.

"So," continued Conner, poker-faced, "what's the news?"

"How should I know?" said Julie, wishing this stupid, belabored dialogue would end. "This is dumb," she dared to mumble.

Despite the crowd noise, Conner overheard her comment. "*Dumb*, Miss Lamar? Did you say this is dumb?"

After another quick burst of laughter, the class fell silent. Everyone watched as Conner and Julie locked stares. "This is not dumb, Miss Lamar," said Conner evenly. "This is a chance for you to show some imagination, some creative thinking. Can you see that, Miss Lamar?"

Julie didn't answer.

"Watch now, Miss Lamar. Here's how it's done. Kevin Ellison!" shouted Conner.

"Yo!" said Ellison, popping up from his perpetual slouch, sitting straight as a West Point plebe.

"Mr. Ellison, if the news was bad, why would someone wait until after supper to tell it?"

"Maybe the guy didn't want to ruin the meal," offered Ellison.

"What if he wasn't that considerate?"

"Then maybe he hated the whole bunch of 'em, including his mother, who hassles him all the time. And he wanted to tell 'em off when it would hurt the most. Maybe he wanted to see 'em all barf royal, you know?"

"Barf royal?" repeated Conner as laughter rippled across the back of the room.

"Yeah. Like upchuck. Buick city."

That comment brought another explosive guffaw.

"There, Miss Lamar," said Conner, once again turning his attention to Julie. "You see what I mean? You're being called on to make an imaginative leap, to see more than you're supposed to see. Do you always do just what you're supposed to do? Just what you've been told to do?"

"I guess."

"Well, now you're being asked to do more."

"Why me?" asked Julie defiantly.

"Why not you?" countered Mr. Conner. He let another moment go by before saying, "For tomorrow, Miss Lamar, I want you to rise to the challenge. I want you to write a one-page essay telling me all about the news. What was it? Why was it important, and so on. Okay?"

Julie looked off as her classmates sat noncommittally waiting for her answer.

"Are you capable of such an extraordinary effort, Miss Lamar?"

Julie shrugged.

"Is that yes?"

Julie looked him dead in the eye, but she didn't intimidate him at all. His persona was seamless.

"Are you nodding yes, Miss Lamar?" asked Conner. "Do I see your head going up and down? If so, your gesturing must be more pronounced to constitute effective communication." With that, Conner dropped the matter and resumed covering the work sheet.

Expressionless, Julie looked down at her work sheet, struggling inwardly to figure out what was happening. The rest of the hour passed uneventfully as her classmates plodded through the remaining sentences. When the bell finally rang, mercifully ending another anxious period for the unprepared, the group thundered out of the room faster than they ever did for a fire drill. Julie was the last to leave. As she neared the door she glanced back at Conner with a questioning look on her face.

"The table is set," he whispered, "and our guests are ready. Do you still want to serve as hostess and dish up something good for them?"

Suddenly it dawned on her. The psychodrama had already begun. Conner had never told her exactly how or when he would set the stage or start the action, but obviously, thought Julie, this was it. She gave a quick nod and walked out of the room.

Once in the hallway, she was surprised to find Craig Morris waiting for her. Craig and she had worked together on the student council last year as well as in the spring play. He too had had a supporting role, and he was very good. She respected him for that, for succeeding so well as an actor that people ignored his looks and simply believed in his character. His soothing, resonant voice and poised demeanor made people like Julie forget about his myopic red eyes, big ears, uncontrollably stiff brown hair, and relative chinlessness. None of that mattered.

41

During rehearsals Julie and Craig managed to have some revealing talks while waiting in the wings for their cues. She'd found out that his parents were also divorced, but that he was living with his father *and* his new wife *and* her three delinquent kids. "Be happy you're alone, Julie," he once said. "You never appreciate it till it's gone."

Now he edged closer to her. "You gonna write it?" he asked.

"What?"

"That challenge essay, or whatever Conner called it."

"I don't know. I don't think so."

"How come?"

"Because nobody else has to do one."

"He won't let you off. You know that."

"You don't think so?"

"I think he's using you to set us up for something else, something bigger. That'd be like him, Mr. Showtime."

"But he's just picking on me," Julie persisted.

"Uh-uh. He embarrasses so many people you can't really say he picks on anyone in particular. Can you see where that leads?"

"What are you doing, defending him?"

"No, not at all. I'm just saying that if I were you I'd slap something together, do some kind of joke essay to let him make his point. Probably sooner or later everybody'll get in the game."

"No," said Julie, warming to her part. "It's not right for him to have his fun at my expense. I don't like being singled out when I haven't done anything wrong. You know there's just a few of us who come prepared for that class every day and work hard."

"Yeah, I know," said Craig in his calming baritone. "It doesn't seem right to me either. But I'm sure Mr. Conner knows what he's doing. Nothing happens by accident

42

in there, right? Everything in class leads to something, some point. Besides, if you don't do this essay, I bet he'll make it harder or longer."

"He wouldn't dare."

"Conner wouldn't dare? Are you kidding?"

"I see what you mean," Julie said with a strained smile. "He is kind of ruthless, isn't he."

"Ruthless," Craig repeated, nodding.

"Well, I still don't know. I have lots of other homework tonight. We've got that unit test in physics tomorrow. So maybe I'll write it, maybe I won't."

"You do what you have to," said Craig, looking at his watch. "But if it were me . . . well, gotta go. Be good."

"Bye Craig," said Julie. As she rushed toward her fourth-hour math class she tried to imagine what Mr. Conner expected. He'd told her that during the course of the psychodrama she would have opportunities to influence the plot and that she should make the most of them. Her decisions, he'd said, would make the play more interesting both for the audience and the actors. By the time she arrived at calculus, she'd concluded that Mr. Conner would expect a conscientious, traditional response on the challenge essay. But by third hour tomorrow, she would produce something quite different.

At lunch Julie discovered no shortage of Advice Givers:

"He's just a slicko blowhard, Julie. He thinks he's God's gift to the world. When he asks for the essay tomorrow, just tell him to shove it." That was Gail Gottshalk's opinion, and Gail's opinions were not to be taken lightly. Hers was a threatening presence. Bright and outspoken, she stood 5 feet 11 inches and weighed in at a solid 165. She was the reigning state champion in the girl's shotput. "Just tell him to stick it where the sun doesn't shine," Gail added with a graphic gesture, guffawing loudly.

Willowy Mary Artis, on the other hand, whose insightful observations about people and their problems had earned her the nickname "Shrink," pointed out that "eighty percent of what Mr. Conner does is for his own amusement. He does what he does to keep from getting bored. To me, it's worth a great deal to have him *not* bored. I find him immensely entertaining when he's not bored. So write the dumb essay, Julie. Spare the man from boredom. It'll be in everybody's interest, believe me."

Julie felt suddenly shaken, unsure of herself and her decision to enter the psychodrama. She was beginning to see that for her to gain something from it, she would have to risk losing everything else, like the trust and respect of people she admired. She thought of the many long bus rides she'd shared with Gail last spring on the way to and from track meets. Gail was so refreshingly honest and funny. And so comfortable now with her commitment to developing the talents she had no matter how "unladylike" they seemed to anyone else. Deceiving Gail was unthinkable.

Deceiving Mary seemed downright impossible. Julie thought Mary was simply too intelligent and too observant to be taken in by the psychodrama. Watching dispassionately with her pale eyes, she was the one who'd catch a teacher making a mistake and tell him about it. "Mr. Dellmar, you're wrong," she'd said last year to the most arrogant member of the English department. "In the book, Holden Caulfield does contemplate suicide." Then she had cited specific references to back her claim.

By day's end Julie had gotten all the coaching on the "Conner problem" she'd ever need. Despite the many pleas to capitulate, to conform, to cooperate, she didn't think finally that the "predictable solution" was really what Mr.

Conner expected. But she also knew he wouldn't be amused by Gail's suggestion. Telling him off that way was too out of character for her. Julie wasn't strong the way Gail was.

By the time she reached home that afternoon, Julie had decided on a sufficiently offbeat solution to her challenge. After another quiet supper alone, she hurried to her room and scribbled out a response to Mr. Conner's assignment. It read:

The solution to the problem is really quite simple. Either the statement is an elliptical construction where the complete sense of it is 'I waited until after supper; then I told my mother the news (was on TV),' or there is a typographical (spelling?) error in the sentence plus an elliptical deletion and the speaker is really saying, 'I waited until after supper; then I told my mother the gnus (were out back eating her rosebushes).'

Julie proofread her effort, folded it, and placed it in her notebook for college prep writing.

CHAPTER
5

The next day Conner let thirty seconds of class time elapse before calling on Julie. "Juliet Lamar," he said loudly, "have you finished your special assignment?"

The group sat motionless, perfectly quiet, everyone waiting anxiously to learn Julie's decision. Because she had shared her strategy with no one, the curiosity of everyone in the room, including Troy Conner, was genuine.

Slowly she nodded.

"Wonderful!" said Conner, beaming. "You're a good citizen after all. What a pleasant surprise. Let's have it."

Julie held out the single sheet of 8½-by-11-inch paper folded lengthwise, and Conner came over and took it from her.

"Very good," he said as he opened the paper and began reading it. He turned and walked toward his desk.

Still no one whispered, no one coughed. Halfway back Conner stopped. He started shaking his head and turned, facing Julie again. "Miss Lamar, Miss Lamar," he said disparagingly, glowering at Julie. "This is, to put it simply, not an acceptable response to the challenge."

Julie didn't react. A couple of rows away she heard two girls whispering frantically.

"This *effort*," he continued, "is too short, too flip, too superficial."

Julie struggled not to smile. She could see Mr. Conner was frowning, but not with his eyes. He'd liked her insolent solution. She could just tell.

"Miss Lamar," he said, "on our first day together didn't I tell this class—which up until now included you— didn't I tell *all* of you that the kind of writing and thinking you relied on in the past just wouldn't be good enough anymore? Didn't I say that for you to make it in this class, you'd have no choice but to grow? Didn't I go through all that?"

"Maybe," mumbled Julie. "I'm sure I don't remember everything said on the first day of class."

Long seconds passed before Conner replied. "Miss Lamar, you're being given a special opportunity to grow, a chance to become more than you are, to see a little more and a little better."

"I don't have time for this," said Julie, liking the role of rebel. "I've got other classes."

"*This*," Conner yelled, shocking everyone to attention, "is not just another class! College prep writing is far more than just another class! It's you, Miss Lamar. It's who you are and who you could become—indeed, will become if you'd only seize your opportunities."

"It's not fair!" Julie contested.

"Look," said Conner, impatience tightening his face

and voice, "let me remind all of you of something. In this course we're concerned not only about the content of your essays but also the content of your character. Before you leave here, before you earn any credit for this, you must know who you are, both in your writing and outside it."

Julie stole a look at her classmates. All eyes were on Conner. His flawless portrayal of a fanatic had entranced them. They believed in him, or they believed that he believed in himself, thought Julie. That was almost as good.

"So, Miss Lamar," he continued, pulling her back to the confrontation, "try to understand that you can't learn the truth until you know the truth of yourself. And the truth shall set you free, remember?"

Julie looked at the floor.

"My point is this," said Conner. "Before the semester ends, all of you will be challenged to determine if you are worthy. To be considered for a passing grade you must accept and meet that challenge. It's like guerrilla warfare— you survive and then you advance. You will be given an assignment that compels you to look into yourself and find that spark of imagination each of you has and that you alone can kindle to a bright, creative flame. For most of you, the spark has been hidden all your short lives. Now you must seek it. Isn't that right, Miss Lamar?" Conner swung around to face Juliet, breaking the spell.

"Whatever you say," she replied.

"What I say, Miss Lamar, is that you must try again . . . and try harder! Since we have our unit test tomorrow, I'll make your second-chance challenge essay due the day after. Only now I want *three* pages, Miss Lamar. Three pages of scintillating prose in which you demonstrate imaginative growth. Do you understand now why I want you to complete this assignment so badly?"

"Why?" asked Julie through clenched teeth.

"Because, to tell you the truth, I still want, more than anything, to know exactly what kind of news someone would wait until *after* supper to tell his or her mother."

Surprisingly, nobody laughed. Julie took that as a good sign. The class, it seemed, was siding with her, empathizing with her plight—secretly thrilled, probably, that it wasn't one of them on the spot. Still, the thought of being found out, of abusing their trust and getting caught at it, frightened Julie.

"So will you accept grace, Miss Lamar?"

Julie glared down at her books, pretended to curse under her breath.

Conner's response was to escalate his attack. "Miss Lamar, didn't you tell me once you wanted to get an A in here? Didn't you write that on the questionnaire I handed out during our first week together? Didn't you ask 'What do I have to do to get an A?' Didn't you?"

Julie refused to answer, refused to even look at him.

"This is wonderful," said Conner. "This is really charming. What have I done, anyway? I've asked someone who supposedly aspires to be an A student to take two steps off dead-center Westpark mediocrity and use her imagination. And what do I get? I get surliness, belligerence, negativism, outright orneriness."

Now Julie had all she could do to keep from breaking up.

"Tell him to cram it," whispered Kevin Ellison from the corner of his mouth.

With that, Julie lost her concentration and laughed.

"Is this funny, Miss Lamar? Is that how you're choosing to treat the assignment? As a joke?"

Julie couldn't face Mr. Conner. She knew she'd lose it again and maybe ruin his control, too. He'd always liked to laugh at her laughing.

"The ball," said Conner, "is in your court, Miss Lamar. The choice, whatever it will be, is yours. You have your orders." Conner stood silently for ten long seconds, but Julie didn't look up to see what he was doing. She guessed he was staring at her with contempt. "Let's move on," he finally said, heading for his desk and the photocopied student essays they were to analyze that hour.

Again, throughout the school day, Julie was besieged by advisors and strategists. At this point in the psychodrama, class opinion was decidedly, even overwhelmingly, in her favor. Despite Conner's promise to assign everyone a challenge essay, Julie was viewed as picked on because she'd been the first to get one.

"Go to the principal about him, or tell another teacher what he's doing. I'm sure it can't be legal," said Margot Clark, a quiet, conscientious student who'd been in lots of Julie's classes since tenth grade. They'd been lab partners in chemistry as juniors, badminton partners in phys ed the year before. At the end of last year Margot had thanked Julie for being so helpful and patient. "I know I'm shy and a lousy conversationalist," she'd said. "But I really liked talking and working with you, okay?"

Mary Artis described Margot as a "viewer, not a doer," but Julie argued the point. "You don't know her, Mary," Julie had said. And Mary let it go at that.

But now, to get so strong a response from someone as timid as Margot, the psychodrama must have hit nerves, deep ones. Julie's doubts multiplied. When the school bell at the end of the day sounded, Julie felt a good deal less certain about her willingness to take on the pressure of the psychodrama. Already she'd lied to so many casual acquaintances and even good friends that she wasn't sure anymore where reality ended and the illusion of the psychodrama began. What would they think, the ones she respected, if they discovered her duplicity. All she had won at Westpark would be lost forever.

Despite their agreement not to talk again until after D day, Julie decided she had to see Mr. Conner one more time. She went to the library after school and hid in the stacks until the building had emptied. Then, making sure nobody saw her, she hurried to Mr. Conner's room. Once there, she scanned the corridors for stragglers; spotting none, she knocked softly on the door. Mr. Conner answered promptly.

"Did anyone see you come here?"

Julie shook her head, then stepped quickly into the room. Conner closed the door, locked it. For a few seconds she stared anxiously at him.

"What's the matter?" he asked.

She couldn't say. She couldn't find the right words, a place to begin.

"You confided in somebody," he guessed. "You told?"

Julie turned her head slowly, but still said nothing.

"You want reassurance."

"I guess," Julie whispered.

"Ahhhhh," said Conner softly, gently taking Julie by the elbow and leading her farther into the quiet room. Finally he stopped and faced her, resting his hands on her shoulders. "I don't think I can give you that," he said. "Not total assurance."

Julie gave him a questioning look.

"In a deal like this, Juliet, nobody can have it all wrapped up. There's an element of chance involved here that has a life of its own. We've put ourselves in a world of intrigue and illusion where uncertainty is the normal state. Understand?"

Julie asked, "Why?"

"Why what?"

"Why are we putting ourselves in a world of illusion?" Her question was sincere.

"Because it's more . . . interesting," said Conner. "And revealing."

Julie nodded and tried to put on a brave smile. Mr. Conner seemed to know it all. He seemed so sure of himself. She still had profound doubts concerning the whole thing.

"The choice is yours," Conner pointed out, taking his hands from her shoulders and burying them in his pockets. He took a step back. "We don't have to go through with it. We can scrub it now if you like. After D day, though, it'll be too late." He allowed a tense silence to build before asking, "What do you want to do?" He stood there immobile, waiting patiently for Julie's answer.

She took her time. She thought of what could be gained from this experience, and what could be lost. If she got caught in the act, she'd probably lose some honest friendships and lots of admiration and respect. But if she backed out now, she might be sacrificing her relationship with Mr. Conner, the first adult to give her back what her own father had taken away—the inspiration to reach up and out, to think big, to take risks.

So she chose. "I want to go ahead with it," she said at last. "Don't ask me why."

"*Why* is always your business," Conner replied.

"Okay."

"Don't worry, you'll be fine. I'm sure of it."

"Wish *I* could be."

"Why aren't you? You've been wonderful so far, a real talent."

"Oh, I don't know."

"Well, you should."

She shrugged.

"So it's set?"

"Yes," Julie replied.

"The day after tomorrow?"

"Yes."

She started for the door.

"Let me go out first," suggested Conner. "If the coast is clear, I'll double back and knock once. Then you take off, okay?"

"Sure," said Julie, although at the time she was sure of very little.

Conner stepped out, closing the door behind him. In less than fifteen seconds Julie heard the single knock. Her hand was on the knob, but when she opened the door and slipped into the hall, she was amazed to find it completely empty. Like a sorcerer, Mr. Conner had vanished into thin air.

CHAPTER
6

At dawn on D day Julie woke up feeling vaguely nauseated. Despite her experience as a performer before many audiences, despite her life as a public person at Westpark, she'd never before felt so nervous. After another drowsy minute she climbed out of bed, stretched, ran her fingers through her long brown hair, and wandered over to a window.

Even in the pinkness of a quiet sunrise, she could see the day was going to be beautiful. It had been unseasonably warm throughout the fall, and there was still no snow on the ground. Gazing a little longer at the soft, stationary morning clouds, Julie began to feel soothed and relaxed. She was sure she could enjoy her shower and keep down her breakfast.

In the kitchen her mother said, "You were yelling in your sleep last night. Woke me up."

Julie froze. "What'd I say?"

"What do you think you said?" asked her mother, her green eyes narrowing. "You feeling guilty?"

"Did I say anything or what?" Julie was struggling not to sound too anxious or annoyed.

"No, don't worry. Nothing I could understand, anyway. It's just you haven't done that since . . . "

Her mother stopped, let the sentence fade.

But Julie finished it: "The divorce." That summer Julie woke up two or three times a week screaming for her father.

"I'm sorry, Julie. I didn't—"

Julie cut in, "I'm a little nervous, I guess."

"Why?"

"I don't know," she lied, losing another measure of self-respect.

Her mother changed the subject, asked instead about her schedule after school, told Julie that she herself had a "business date" that evening. When her mother left the table to dress, Julie thought about her own business date, the psychodrama.

The day before had been test day in college prep writing, a quiet and totally uneventful class period. Mr. Conner hadn't talked to her, hadn't singled her out in any way, hadn't even looked at her. Julie knew she'd done well on the sentence-classification test; others complained about how the tense and intimidating atmosphere distracted them. Julie almost wished she could warn them about the distraction they'd face today.

At school Julie was asked no less than twenty times by different people whether she'd written her second challenge essay. Each time she'd answered ambiguously, saying, "Not yet, but I'll have a challenge for him by class time."

Mary Artis was the first to push Julie for more. "Specifics, Julie, c'mon!" she'd said. "What're you going to do exactly?"

"Really, I haven't decided."

"Then let's decide now, okay? I mean, there we are in class. Mr. Conner takes roll, turns to you, and says, 'Miss Lamar, how about it?' Then you say . . ." Mary held out her hand, prompting Julie. "C'mon, Julie, take it!"

Julie hesitated, then lied again, "I don't know yet."

Mary said, "Hmmm," eyeing Julie skeptically.

She knows, thought Julie. Panicking, Julie said, "Gotta run, okay?"

Mary said nothing, just continued to stare.

Finally, third hour arrived. Julie walked anxiously into the classroom. She felt so self-conscious that she dared not look at anyone. She was afraid she would be tempted to quit. She had been seated less than a minute when Conner broke the uneasy silence.

"Say, Miss Lamar," he began in a taunting way, looking at her with hooded eyes. Then he pretended to search for something on his desk, moving around piles of photocopied essays and work sheets, sliding aside a fat dictionary and a half-read novel, even lifting his desk-mat calendar and peeking underneath.

"Miss Lamar," he said, "I seek, but I don't find."

"Pardon?" said Julie.

"Did you complete the challenge essay, Miss Lamar? Did you rise to the occasion and decide to be something more than a member of the mediocre majority?"

Julie slowly shook her head.

"Is that really *no*, Miss Lamar? NO?" he called out, raising his voice theatrically.

"No, I didn't do it," she answered, her eyes burning dully.

They glared at each other a few seconds. His stare was unexpectedly fierce. Then Conner scanned the rest of the class, found them watching openmouthed or looking down at their desktops, surly frowns in place.

"Miss Lamar," said Conner, returning his attention to Julie (who'd put on a convincing look of slit-lidded hate), "Miss Lamar," he said quietly, his voice full of false pity, "have you ever heard the old expression 'Go with the flow'?"

Julie sat stonefaced, silent.

"Well, have you ever heard that—'Go with the flow'?"

"Yes, I've heard that," she said finally.

"Know what it means?"

She nodded, rolling her eyes in frustration.

"Well, Miss Lamar, in here, in this room, in this class, I . . . *direct* the flow." Conner spoke softly, spacing his words in a deliberate and disarming way. "That's my job. Your job," he continued, "is to go with the flow. And you really should go with it. You'd be a lot happier. Because, Miss Lamar, those who choose *not* to go with the flow . . . just go. *Comprende?*"

Julie tracked him with a hostile gaze and refused to comment. She didn't move a muscle.

"Let me speak even more plainly, then," pushed Conner. "If you don't join the class today, Miss Lamar, it'll have to be the old *adios* syndrome for you. *Terminus attendus*, understand? So what'll it be? Are you going to go with the flow? Or just go?"

"That's no choice at all, is it," argued Julie. Then in a whiny voice she asked, "Know what?"

"No, what?" Conner replied, skillfully mimicking Julie's nyah-nyah tone.

"I've had it with you and this class and all the harassment. It's not fair at all!" With that, she stood up and marched toward the door.

"Well, let's not panic," taunted Conner. "I mean, really. There's a time to fight, and there's a time to flow. But I guess guys know more about it than girls, right?"

That was her cue to begin the one scene they'd practiced. Without saying another word, Julie pushed open the door, took a half step back into the room, spun toward Conner, and hurled her bulky Warriner's *English Grammar* book point-blank at his head. In trying to duck the flying text, Conner lost his balance and fell off his swivel chair, landing on a stack of two boxes holding old student papers and tests. He collapsed the boxes with the force of his fall. The others gasped.

Running out the door and down the hall, Julie knew Mr. Conner would be on his feet and after her in a second. He would jump into the hallway and make a big show of trying to determine which direction she'd gone. When he had done enough looking to convince the other students his shock was authentic, he would reenter the room. Once back inside, he would go into his prepared speech about how upset he was with this incident. He would explain that he had used these "motivational tactics" for years to "liberate adolescent imaginations." Mostly he would plead with them to keep the problem within the class. He'd request they mention the blowup to no one. "Give me a few days to figure out what happened here," he'd say.

Then, after an appropriate pause, he would tell them he needed their ideas, too. So he would ask them all to take out a piece of paper and write an analysis, a summary. They would be asked to explain how they thought the problem had developed and what could be done about it now. He would also ask that they tell him anything they could about Julie. "Is there something going on with her I should be made aware of?" he would say.

After collecting the responses, Conner would ask if anyone had other classes with Julie. If he found someone who did, and he knew he would, he'd ask that person to tell Julie to see him before the day was over. It was Conner's job to appear shaken and shocked. He also wanted to seem paranoid about the possibility that the confrontation could get him in Big Trouble with the Office, Dolten & Company.

Conner must have played his part well, for throughout the day Julie was told again and again, hour after hour, that Mr. Conner wanted to see her "as soon as possible!" When Mary and Craig talked to her, they were surprisingly nonjudgmental, as if they didn't want to pick sides just yet, or worse, pick the wrong side. Only Gail said, "Good goin', Julie. The SOB had it comin' all the way!"

Again Julie went to the library after school and waited for the last of the students to leave. When she was certain she could make it to Conner's room unseen, she left the stacks to report in. She knocked just once before Conner opened up.

Quickly he pulled her in and shut the door. They both took another step into the room before turning to face each other. Instantly they burst out laughing, and Conner threw a careless arm around her shoulders and hugged her to him, a jubilant coach. Then he released her and stepped aside.

"You were wonderful!" he said. "I nearly believed you myself. It was a flawless blending of rebellion and resolve. And you timed your surprise for them perfectly."

"Thanks," she said, feeling exhilarated by the response of her audience, by the success of the psychodrama. "It was fun. I really got into it."

"Assault on a certified teaching professional?"

"That was the easy part."

Conner then told her about how expertly she'd placed her shot. "The book came in head-high, and I was able to take it on the forearm just as we'd planned. It was by far the best throw you ever made, the best you could've made!"

Julie watched his face. His smile seemed genuinely warm, but now she saw a glint of sardonic amusement in his eyes, which held her for a long second.

"I've got a question," she said. "Last night I tried to call you."

He raised his eyebrows a fraction as if she'd surprised him. "And?"

"And nobody knew your number. Nobody knows it. It's like you don't exist outside this place."

"Or maybe that's when I finally do exist," said Conner. He was still smiling, but barely.

"How come?"

"How come what?"

"Why have an unlisted number?"

A prolonged silence followed Julie's question. Then Conner mumbled something to himself before his eyes sought hers. "It's like this," he began. "I'm very concerned about keeping what I am here separate from what I want to be away from here. You see, this is not my home, my world. It's your home. This place belongs to the students, the spoils of war. I'm just a refugee. I'm only passing through. Maybe to you it seems just the opposite."

"What's the opposite?"

"That you're the one who's passing through while I'm destined to stay for the duration."

"Won't you? Don't I get to leave a lot sooner than you?"

"You may think so."

"I don't get it."

"You will. Just know that I do have an escape plan for myself. And you've helped me with it."

"How?"

"Can't say."

Julie looked off, then asked, "Why do you tease me so much?"

"I'm not teasing you."

"Why all the secrecy then? Are you afraid someone's going to egg your house or something?" Julie slid him a wary smile.

Conner tilted his head and looked at her obliquely. "It's simple. I don't like to be taken for granted. I don't like to be used. So many of my colleagues let that happen to themselves. With the unlisted number, the district bosses have to work even to have a conversation with me. It's petty, but it's what I can do." He nodded as though he'd just revealed the meaning of life.

"I still don't get it," Julie said.

"I know. I don't either sometimes. Anything else?" said Conner, discouraging Julie from asking if he really did live "way out by a lake someplace."

"Now what?" she asked instead.

"The forces are in motion."

"Meaning?"

"It's out of our hands."

"But what should I do tomorrow?"

"Don't come to class. Just stay lost for the hour. I'm not quite done working on them yet."

"Who?"

"Your classmates."

"Oh, okay."

"Here's something," he said, walking over to his desk. "While you're gone, you might want some informative reading."

Julie watched as he pulled a bulging manila envelope from beneath the desk. He held it out to her.

"What's this?"

"The responses. They're pretty entertaining."

"Yeah? Why?"

"They tell of a changing girl who is sending mixed signals to her friends."

"Which signals to which friends?"

"Here," he said, offering her the envelope. "You try making sense of them."

"Can I?" she asked, suddenly tentative.

"You've got their respect, though. I'll say that much," Conner added. "They don't know quite what to do with you. They can't find a category, a label."

Julie didn't know what to say, but she looked forward to reading the responses.

"Any last questions?" asked Conner, looking at his watch.

"You're in a hurry," Julie said.

"Today I am."

"Okay, I'm leaving. And I should skip class tomorrow?"

"That's what it'll amount to. Fate has decreed that you vanish."

As Julie left the room she didn't quite know how to interpret the distracted gleam in Mr. Conner's eyes or the triumphant half-smile on his face. Was he sneering at her?

CHAPTER
7

That night Julie was home alone again.

"I won't be too late, honey," her mother had said just before leaving.

"Who is he?" asked Julie.

"A teacher."

"Oh, yeah?"

"Well, a professor actually."

"Where?"

"The university."

"What does he teach?"

"Psychology. I interviewed him. We needed some expert testimony on job stress for a suit one of our clients is bringing against an airline."

"Is he handsome?" Julie was teasing, but she didn't think her mother knew it.

"He's respectable." Before Julie could ask anything else, her mother said, "Be good. Mind the store."

"You too," Julie called as she closed the door and snapped shut the dead bolt. Ever since her mother had resumed dating, Julie could find herself alone any night of the week, not just Friday or Saturday. She had mixed feelings about her mother's social life. While she thought it natural for an attractive woman like her mother to have male friends and to develop "adult relationships" with them, she also resented her mother's becoming less a mother and more a roommate to her.

Too often lately, her mother had talked to Julie as a peer, a frazzled adolescent beset by dating problems, makeup decisions, clothing choices—the whole silly business. Too often Julie was unwillingly cast in the role of parent, of advisor to the lovelorn. And too often, or so she thought at first, her mother had abandoned her, left her to fend for herself during hard times. "I can't hide behind my glasses forever, Julie," her mother said recently. "I've got to have some fun in life, too. I can't just let it slip away, and that's exactly what I've been doing. Can you understand that?"

Julie had said she would try.

After her mother left, Julie went up to her room, sat down at her desk, and opened the manila envelope Mr. Conner had given her. She pulled out the papers and began reading through them, getting a little upset by the way some of her classmates had perceived her and her behavior in the psychodrama. Even though there were no names on the papers, she recognized the handwriting on some of them. But not on the first one, which began:

I don't know what's going on in this class sometimes. One thing I do know is that Julie Lamar is a very conscientious

student and a sensitive person. She takes things very per-
sonally. I think she reacted the way she did to the challenge
essay for a couple of reasons. One, I'm sure she thinks
she's being picked on because she was the first of us to get
the assignment and because she's so intelligent. But she
did make a try at it. So why not just drop everything and
leave her alone? Second, I think Julie's been having a hard
time relating to her friends recently. They're a little con-
fused because she doesn't want to do the same kinds of
things they've always done in the past. She knows kids
from lots of cliques but right now she doesn't seem to be
close to anybody. To solve the problem, Julie should apol-
ogize and you, Mr. Conner, should just forget all the sar-
castic showboating. We don't know when you're serious
and when you aren't. Lots of kids in here feel confused
and even scared. Why not just tell us what you want and
do some real teaching instead of this kind of useless har-
assment? What gives you the right to play power games
with us anyway? I think you use scare tactics like this just
to keep us beneath you. Do you feel threatened or some-
thing? You really should show us some respect.

"Take that, Mr. Conner," Julie said out loud. But as
she looked back over this statement, she felt anxious, even
guilty. Had she hurt the people she liked by concentrating
too much on the future? Should she have been more subtle
about her goals? More gracious to her friends?

She quickly shuffled that paper to the bottom of the
stack and read the next one, which offered an entirely
different perspective. It started emotionally with:

My god, but I wish both of you would just grow up! Don't
think I haven't seen how you stare at Julie Lamar when
you think nobody is watching. If you've got the hots for

her, why not just deal with it after school, on your own time! Instead you waste all of our time with your cutesy nasty stunts. I don't know why Julie Lamar threw the book at you, but if you're not careful I'm going to go find some lawyer who'll do the same thing! As of now, as far as I know, you're only guilty of humiliating Julie. Don't try taking it any further. Just do the job you're paid to do.

This irate response made Julie realize what Mr. Conner meant when he said the psychodrama would cost them plenty, that it was dangerous, that it would change them forever. For one short moment she was afraid. She felt she'd been drawn into something much darker, far more sinister than she'd first imagined.

As she read over the rest of the statements, she discovered that most fell somewhere between the extremes of the first two. Of course it didn't really matter what she thought of her classmates anymore, or what they thought of her. She was far past the point of no return. She realized now she could no longer step out of the psychodrama. That left her dependent on one person. But she was sure of Mr. Conner, and he believed in her.

Julie was in a deep sleep when the phone rang. As she reached for it, she squinted at her glowing clock radio. It was nearly 2:00 A.M. Since moving into the apartment, Julie and her mother had received three or four obscene calls, but the threat of getting others wasn't strong enough yet to force them to unplug the phone at night or get an unlisted number. Julie slowly picked up the receiver and brought it to her ear. "Hello," she said tentatively.

"Maybe you can fool most of 'em," said a male voice in a raspy whisper, "but not me."

"Who is this?" she asked quickly, her mind racing to match the voice with some boy she knew.

"It's a con job, a setup, right?"

"Who's calling?" she said, still trying for a positive identification.

"I knew it!" growled the voice. "Jus' remember—more than one can play, huh?"

"What are you talking—"

"Shut up! You sold out, you pay." Before Julie could speak again, the line went dead. Tight with rage, Julie slammed down the receiver. Now she was angry at herself for being unable to guess who'd called. The noise woke her mother.

"Julie?" she murmured sleepily from across the hall.

"It's okay. I just bumped the telephone," said Julie. She waited for a response but didn't get one. Apparently her mother had already fallen back asleep.

The next day, Wednesday, Julie did as Mr. Conner suggested. She skipped third hour and disappeared in the library. That was the safest place in the school to hide because it was big, cluttered, and understaffed.

During her first and second periods nobody said much to Julie about the scene. And she knew why. Conner had invoked the gag rule.

Halfway through fourth-hour math, however, Julie was called out of class by an office aide. "Here," said the short, stocky, wispy-haired girl, an eleventh grader.

"What is it?" Julie asked, taking the note. Before the other girl could answer, Julie saw exactly what it was—a detention slip. She'd been ordered to serve her time either after school today or tomorrow. Confused, Julie returned to her class while the office aide drifted silently down the hall.

At the end of the day Julie opted not to serve detention but to serve notice on Mr. Conner. She quickly disengaged herself from a conversation with Gail and Mary, whose lockers were near hers, and hurried instead to Mr. Conner's room. She was again able to enter unseen.

Conner looked at his watch when she walked in on him. This time he didn't even get up to close the door. She pulled it shut herself before asking, "What's going on?"

"What do you mean?" he answered in a flat, preoccupied voice, his arms folded across his chest. He offered her a small, stiff smile.

"Why'd you give me detention?" she asked. "What's the plan?" Julie knew she sounded irritated, whiny.

"At this point," he said, "the plan is whatever happens. The plot is out of our hands now. I told you that. We started things in motion, but now all we can do is what's logical and natural."

"Who's in control?"

"Who knows, ultimately?"

"Back to detention," said Julie. "Why'd you give it to me?"

"You skipped my class," he answered, completely serious. "Your absence was unexcused."

"But you told me to skip!" There was an unguarded quaver in her voice.

"Did I really?" A sarcastic little frown creased his forehead.

"Yes!" Julie asserted, aggravated now by the mocking look Conner was giving her. "What am I supposed to—"

He brought his hand up, silencing her. "If I'd done nothing, if I hadn't reported you, would you expect to be able to walk unchallenged back into a class where the day before you'd thrown a book at the teacher? Wouldn't you expect some consequence for your behavior? Wouldn't your classmates expect your act to have consequences?"

Julie thought a moment before reluctantly conceding. "Yeah, I s'pose."

"I *s'pose*, too. In fact one hour of detention would seem the very least you could expect, right?"

"If you say so."

"What do *you* say? Can you think of a more natural plot line?"

"No." An awkward silence passed. "I just think I'd enjoy everything more if I knew what it meant. If I knew what you wanted from me. I can't believe you expect me to stand here and thank you for giving me only an hour of detention."

Conner smiled and shrugged.

"What do I do now? I need a sense of direction," said Julie.

"Take another day off," said Conner, leaning back, staring at the ceiling.

"Are you crazy?" she snapped.

"Not at all."

"I don't believe this."

"You're not alone there. I think we have some doubters in class."

"Mary Artis," said Julie.

"You think so?"

"Don't you?"

"I haven't mentioned a name yet. Why Mary? Has she said something?"

"No, she's just too smart to buy into this."

"We'll see."

"Somebody called me late last night," Julie blurted.

Conner swung around and stared directly into her eyes, probing (thought Julie) for something—some fear, some weakness, some secret. "When?" he asked, squinting in concentration.

"Two in the morning."

"And?"

"He said this was all fake. A con job was how he put it."

"Who said?" Conner frowned and looked puzzled.

"I don't know. I tried to keep him talking, but he hung up on me."

"You have no idea who it was?" His eyes were nervous and alert now.

"I've been listening all day, but I can't find the voice."

"Did you admit anything about our little project?"

"You think I'm crazy?"

"Are you?"

"I must be to have gotten involved in this."

"C'mon," Conner said softly.

"I'm confused," Julie said.

"If you weren't doing things you don't understand just now, you wouldn't be confused."

"Huh?" Julie replied, a reluctant half-smile brightening her face a little.

"I told you this would be expensive, didn't I?"

"You mean I have to pay with more phone calls, more detention?"

"No," he answered curtly. Then he asked, "How did you like those papers?"

"Interesting. What did you think?" She smiled fully for the first time since entering Conner's room. She was recalling the rebukes aimed at him.

"I have my enemies, don't I?" he commented.

"You knew you would."

"Certainly. And it's only natural that they'll side with one of their own at first."

"Uh-huh."

"See? It's going to cost me, too," he said, nodding vigorously. "Any comments today from friends?"

"Nope. You must've really scared them after I took off. I think they're even afraid to talk to each other."

"I did my best."

By this point Julie's anger had subsided. Mr. Conner's explanations seemed reasonable enough, so she felt buoyant again, able to cope.

"Hey, look," said Conner, "I have to throw you out now. I have a meeting to attend."

Julie began heading for the door. "Bye," she said.

Conner didn't answer. He merely stood there, smiling, but holding the smile too long, like someone who knew the latest gossip or some dark personal secret and wasn't about to reveal it.

Julie stared back at him, shook her head, and walked out.

That evening Julie was again by herself. This time her mother was staying overnight in Duluth, where she was attending a two-day computer seminar. So when the phone rang, shattering the late-hour silence and Julie's efforts to finish her math homework, she wanted to let it ring itself out.

Finally, cautiously, she reached for the receiver. "Hello?" she said.

"Julie?"

"Yes." The voice was familiar, not last night's voice.

"Sorry to call so late."

Julie glanced at the clock and was surprised that it was already ten-thirty. She said nothing.

"Julie, it's me, Craig. Craig Morris."

"Oh, Craig," said Julie with obvious relief, her voice wavering.

"Something wrong?"

"No, I'm just nervous. I've been working on math for too long. It's been too quiet. The phone startled me."

"Oh."

"What's new?"

"Huh?"

"Why'd you call?"

"Well, I wanted to talk to you about Conner."

"What about him?" She tried to speak in a neutral tone.

"Maybe it's none of my business, and if that's how you feel, just say so—"

"What's on your mind, Craig?"

"I guess I'm wondering why you're letting this challenge essay thing get so out of hand. I mean, it's not like you at all."

"What isn't like me?"

"To get so upset the way you did, then skip class, then have detention. People are talking."

"What are they saying?"

"Plenty. Ol' Shauna Saunders volunteered to be third-shift foreman at the rumor mill."

Julie laughed. "So what're you, the social conscience of Westpark? The chief negotiator?"

"I'm your friend, I think," he replied, "aren't I?"

"Yes."

"How come, then?"

"How come what?"

"Why don't you just talk to Mr. Conner? He likes you. You know that. He respects your work."

"Are you advising me to do the challenge essay?"

"I'm not advising you to do anything but look out for your own best interests."

"What are my best interests?"

"Getting credit for college prep writing might be one."

"It might be."

"I bet Conner wants this to end as much as you do. As much as the rest of the class does."

"What if I don't want it to end? What if I can't end it?"

Craig allowed an uncomfortable silence to stretch before he said, "Maybe I was right. Maybe it is none of my business."

"I know what you're doing, and I appreciate it," said Julie.

"But . . ."

"But I don't know what to think sometimes."

"I do."

"And?"

"Drop it, Julie. It's a waste of your time. It's a lost cause. Make peace and survive."

After saying good-bye, Julie carefully replaced the receiver, unsure of herself again. Craig's advice was appealing. Quitting would simplify things, if only it were possible to do. But she was also beginning to see that she'd become involved in something so unique it made her unique. And she didn't want to lose that.

At school on Thursday, Julie did as she'd been told. She skipped third-hour college prep writing and again hid in the library. She consciously avoided being anywhere near Conner's room so that her friends couldn't buzz around her between classes and bombard her with whys. Instead, she waited until the last possible moment to race to fourth-hour math.

She hadn't been seated five minutes before Ms. Mortenson, her calculus teacher, was again interrupted by a knock at the door. Again, it was the chubby office assistant. Again, the matter concerned Juliet Lamar. Again, Julie was called out of class. But this time, unlike yesterday, she was not simply served a detention slip. Instead, she received a *"See me immediately!"* summons from Mr. William Wright, vice-principal.

"He wants to talk to you *now*," the aide said before continuing her rounds.

Nervous and alarmed, Julie walked quickly to the administrative wing. On arriving, she was taken directly to Mr. Wright's office. She stood in the doorway and looked at him as he read over the disciplinary report on his desk, a report undoubtedly involving her. He didn't acknowledge her presence, but let her wait awkwardly half in, half out of his office.

Julie had seen Wright roaming the halls, but never in her two and a quarter years at Westpark had she spoken to him. She always thought he looked the part of the stern disciplinarian. His close-cropped, thinning reddish hair, his watery, unblinking pale eyes, his florid face, thin mouth, solid thrust of jaw, bull neck, and beefy shoulders all added to his image as an enforcer. Already, after only half a minute, Julie felt intimidated. She cleared her throat to get his attention.

"I see you," he said without moving his lips, his eyes still on the report. "Come in. Sit down." He still hadn't looked at her. Julie quickly followed his orders.

Wright continued reading. Julie's palms perspired. Finally she broke the silence by asking casually, "What's the big deal?"

Still staring at the pink disciplinary form on his desk, Vice-Principal Wright lifted his eyebrows and gazed at Julie over the tops of his steel-rimmed glasses. His skeptical, shrewd eyes were as cold as winter pebbles. "The deal," he replied, "is that Mr. Conner wants me to take you out of his third-hour section of college prep writing."

"He wants to drop me?" said Julie, suddenly short of breath.

"Put you in a study hall," Wright clarified, continuing to stare over his glasses.

In a barely audible voice, her face full of confusion, Julie asked, "Why?"

"That's what I'd like to know," he said, his voice low and not unkind. "I can't quite make sense of his memo. You threw a book at him on Tuesday. Is that right?"

Julie looked down, her lips pressed together. She sat holding her breath, her body tense. She felt trapped and betrayed.

CHAPTER 8

"Is that true?" asked Wright, a look of disbelief crossing his face.

"What?" said Julie glancing up, meeting Mr. Wright's disconcerting gaze, a stare that made her feel guilty for things she'd never done, never even imagined doing.

"Did you throw a book—"

"No, I didn't throw it," interrupted Julie. "I was trying to leave it on his desk. I got mad. I tossed the book, maybe." By now her breathing had become fast and shallow again.

"It hit him."

"No."

"That's what it says here. It says, 'The book struck me high on my left shoulder and ricocheted up to my temple, knocking me off balance.'" Again Wright stared across the desk at Julie, but this time a narrow smile, half calming, half mocking, softened his features. She also saw a look of mild amusement in his eyes. "You hit your teacher with a book?" he asked quietly, incredulously, almost over-acting now.

Julie knew that once again she was at a turning point—a moment of decision. At least that's what she thought at first. But another moment's reflection made her see that there was really no choice. For her to risk calling the psy-chodrama her motivation for throwing a book was to risk seeming not just immature in Wright's eyes, but absurd. Suddenly the truth appeared so ridiculous she chose to stay on the only path open to her. She kept silent about her special relationship with Mr. Conner.

"Do you have any explanation for these actions, young lady?" asked Wright.

"I lost my temper," said Julie. "It was a stupid thing to do."

"And dangerous." Again, the flickering smile.

"Yes," Julie replied.

Wright sat back in his thronelike leather chair. He sighed and stared at a corner of the desk. Finally he said, "Here's what we're going to do. I'm going to put you on a disciplinary contract." He pulled a sheet of paper from one of the side drawers of his desk. "Once you sign this, you may return to class. However, if you fail to follow *any* of the rules listed here, whether it concerns tardiness, missed work, inattentive or insubordinate classroom behavior, that'll be it. You'll lose credit for college prep writing and be assigned to study hall for the rest of the semester."

"What if I don't sign?" ventured Julie.

Now Wright really zeroed in on her with a sharp, hostile stare. "That will result in immediate loss of credit and placement in a study hall," he said.

"I understand," said Julie.

"I knew you would." Mr. Wright pushed the behavior contract across the desk to Julie.

She quickly signed it and stood up. Then she thought to ask, "May I go?"

"You may."

Without looking at Wright, Julie turned to leave.

"Be in class tomorrow," he reminded her.

"I will."

"And do watch out for Mr. Conner, would you? He's much to valuable to lose."

Julie slid a quick look at Wright and again caught a glimpse of a smile, but this time it lingered, just as Mr. Conner's had yesterday. She left the office sensing that the unthinkable had suddenly become possible: *everyone* was in on the psychodrama, and she was now in a situation where anything could happen. For the first time since becoming involved with Mr. Conner, she was *afraid*. All of life, it appeared, had become a conspiracy. After all, wasn't Mr. Conner the Phantom? Hadn't he as much as admitted working with other faculty members to victimize and humiliate students? And couldn't he just as easily convince other students, such as Mary and Craig, to join him in his projects? Hadn't he convinced her?

No sooner had Julie reentered the hallway when she walked right into Shauna Saunders. For once Shauna was without her perpetual accessory, Mike Bryant.

"Oh, I've heard about *you*, girl," Shauna said in an excited whisper as her eyes darted back and forth from Julie's face to the sign over Mr. Wright's office door. As usual, she placed her hand on Julie's forearm, her singular gesture of intimacy, of shared experience and viewpoint. The act couldn't have been less appropriate, thought Julie. "So it's true?" asked Shauna, her face flushed with anticipation. "You can tell me."

"Tell you what?" said Julie, whose ignorance was, for once this week, innocent, unrehearsed.

"About how you and Mr. T.C. are having some kind of lover's quarrel."

At first Julie couldn't even muster a response. She simply rolled her eyes and shook her head. "Shauna," she said finally, "if you're so anxious to find out what goes on in college prep writing, why don't you take the class?"

"Too much hassle. You know I like a flexible schedule. I need lots of free time . . . just like you," Shauna said with an exaggerated wink. "C'mon, now. Tell me about you and the gorgeous Mr. Conner."

"Shauna, you've got too much time on your hands, too much time to think. And too little to think with." Julie surprised herself with that retort. It was one of the most sarcastic remarks she had ever made to someone in public.

But Shauna yammered on as if Julie had just asked for her complete analysis of the situation. She hadn't gotten the message. "It just doesn't look good, Julie. If you were cheering this year, you'd be in real trouble. We just couldn't let you—"

Julie jerked her arm away and stormed off before Shauna could finish. Ten steps later Julie found herself near tears—tears of frustration, tears of anger and hurt. She walked quickly and stared straight ahead, not daring to blink and send the tears coursing down her face. She had no one to turn to. And she couldn't let Shauna see what was happening to her. She wanted to be alone now.

She *was* alone—all alone. That realization jolted her. None of her friends would listen to the "real" truth now, not after she had fooled them all week, had faked a crisis so upsetting that even casual friends offered words of concern and encouragement, at least at first. Whose side were they on now? She saw how Conner had isolated her, cut her off from everyone, even himself. But no, that wasn't true either. She had cut her own ties with friends. She'd been cutting them for some time, though recently she'd done it because she had trusted Conner to give her more, show her something better. And she'd believed in him.

Julie sought refuge in the girls' bathroom, where she tried to regain her composure. If only she could talk to her father. If only he were closer. He would understand what Mr. Conner was up to. He knew about such things, the real world. At least that's what he implied. Didn't he always say, "Julie, when you know what life is like—that you can't just stand still and take it—you'll understand why I'm doing what I'm doing." If only he could be here *now*, thought Julie desperately, he would explain it all, reveal how to win this game.

Soon Julie calmed down enough to return to her fourth-hour class. But she spent the rest of the day anxiously debating whether to confront Mr. Conner again. By the end of the last hour, sick at heart, nearly sick to her stomach, Julie decided she couldn't go home without talking to the only person left for her to trust. Unfortunately, he was also the one who had in less than a week nearly destroyed her capacity to trust.

"I want to know where I am," Julie said as Troy Conner closed the door behind her and followed her into the room. She'd stormed in on him again, but this time he didn't seem surprised or upset. As always, he had his marvelous composure.

"Only you know that, Julie," he answered.

"No, I don't."

"Of course you do," he said indifferently, looking at the floor.

She watched him until he turned and met her gaze.

Giving her a long, probing look, he seated himself and signaled for her to do the same. Julie did so, feeling she was in the grip of a man so skilled at controlling reality that he scared her. But she wasn't about to admit that, even to herself. Instead she gave him her best baleful stare.

"Where am I?" she asked again, her whole being rigid with defiance.

"At Westpark High . . . having the time of your life."

"This is getting out of hand. I've had enough. You've got to stop it."

"I can't stop it. You know that."

"You can too."

"No, Julie. Not now. Not anymore. It has a life of its own now, remember?"

"You just say things like that to sound mysterious and superior. You want me to think you're dangerous."

He smiled. "Do I?"

She glowered at him and then looked down. Was he wise or wicked, visionary or just plain vicious? At that moment Julie couldn't honestly tell. She looked up and studied his face. It betrayed not the least inclination to let her in on the elaborate joke he was playing. She felt used.

"Tell me what to do," she said in a last desperate attempt to find meaning. "Tell me what you're trying to make me do." She spoke softly now and continued searching his eyes for something she could believe in. But his eyes, like his words, gave nothing away.

Finally he said, "Are you going the way of that other wonderfully dramatic Juliet?"

"I don't understand."

"What did that romantic, idealistic young girl do?"

Julie thought back to her sophomore literature class, tried to recall the critical details of the Shakespeare play. "She killed herself."

"Why?"

"For love," she said. "For grief."

"Why was she grief-stricken?"

"Because the trick didn't work. She didn't wake up soon enough."

"Soon enough for what?" Conner prodded patiently.

"Soon enough to save Romeo. To stop him from committing suicide."

"Who else?"

Again Julie felt empty-headed. She looked to Conner for enlightenment, but he looked away. Confused, recollecting nothing relevant, she gave a small shrug.

"Who else didn't she save?" he asked again. "You know."

Then she saw where he was going, where he was taking her. "Herself," Julie whispered. "She didn't wake up in time to save herself."

"Exactly," Conner replied. "Wake up, Juliet," he said with a threatening directness. "Wake up in time to save what's most important."

"Save myself? Is that what I'm supposed to do? How? Save myself from what?" Her strident voice, she realized too late, was betraying her anger.

"Save your belief in yourself," he replied, with an odd little smile. "Don't let anyone take that from you."

Julie waited for more, but he added nothing.

"This is all crazy. Crazy!" she yelled suddenly, standing up, her face burning with humiliation. "You've got no right!"

"No right to what, Juliet?" Conner asked calmly.

"No right to play God the way you do."

"Meaning?"

"Meaning you set up this stupid psychodrama and pulled me into it and made me lie to my friends and made

82

it so I can't tell anybody the truth about this and be believed! And now you're trying to make me lose credit for the class! I mean, what is it with you? Why are you trying so hard to ruin me? What did I ever do to you except try to be your friend?"

Despite her efforts at self-control, Julie couldn't stop angry tears from welling up in the corners of her eyes and spilling down her face. At first she turned her head away and brushed her eyes with the back of her wrist. Then she decided not to hide her face, her feelings. Instead she looked directly at Conner and challenged him with the hurt. "What do you want from me anyway?" she asked.

As she waited for his reaction, things he had said came back to her, all with dreadful double meanings she'd somehow never noticed before.

Conner slowly stood up and stepped closer, lifting his arms and holding them out as if he were going to embrace her. Julie hugged her books with both hands, protecting herself, forbidding Conner to come closer.

"What do you *want*?" she cried, her voice full of fear now.

Conner touched her shoulders, held them gently. "I want to see you far better prepared for life than I was. I want you to have the chance to confront the most important truth I ever learned."

"What gives you the right?" she asked again, her voice less shrill.

"You gave me the right," said Conner. "You chose to enter the psychodrama. I didn't coerce you into it. I didn't make you do anything. You chose to let chance take you where it would. What you must understand, what you must always remember, is that occasionally even chance can be influenced, and you must never neglect to take advantage then. Remember, too, that no one gets sold down the river without in some way wanting to make the trip. So *you* tell *me*—what's in this for you? Why'd you do it?"

"That's what I'm asking. What does it all mean?" Julie replied, keeping her body rigid in his grasp. "I've listened to you long enough to know that what you say can mean lots of different things. But I don't know what *you* mean to me anymore."

"I'm sorry," said Conner softly, staring calmly down at her, his hands still resting on her shoulders. "I want very much to mean something to you."

"So why are you trying to hurt me?"

"I'm not trying to hurt you."

"That's what you're doing no matter what you call it." Another tear slid down her cheek, and she swiped at it with her hand.

"I'm doing exactly what I said I'd do the day you agreed to enter the psychodrama. I'm putting you in a situation where you can discover something important *for* yourself *by* yourself. That's the only kind of learning that counts, the only kind that means anything."

Tears still blurring her vision, Julie looked down. "All I'm learning is that I was wrong to trust you. And I did trust you. I even thought maybe . . ." Once more Julie felt herself losing control. She wept quietly and intensely.

When Conner tried to take her books from her, she let him. He put them down on his desk and turned back to her, embracing her at last, trying to soothe and calm her. And she let him.

"I'm sorry," she said, referring to her lack of self-possession.

"So am I," Conner whispered. "Things haven't turned out very well so far, have they?"

"No," Julie replied, her forehead against Conner's

84

chest, her arms still folded protectively in front of her, her fists under her chin.

"Do you know what I wanted from you since the very beginning?" asked Conner.

"For me to grow," she answered.

"I wanted to make love with you."

Julie froze in his arms. Breathless, she wondered if she should shove him away and run for it, maybe scream for help. Before she could act he continued, "I wanted to make love with your mind. That's what art is, you know. It's love, generosity, sharing. It's not anger and vengeance." Now he took a deep breath. "I gave you the psychodrama because I want to count for something in your life, which is going to be very special. I'm sure of it. I want to be remembered as an artist, as one who helped you make an important discovery."

"What discovery?" Julie asked in a way she hoped would put Conner on guard. Her head knew she shouldn't believe him anymore and that she should leave as fast as she could. But her heart knew something too: She was in this play with him. They were partners. They were creating, sharing a special experience, enjoying a special relationship. "What discovery?" Julie repeated.

"If I told you outright, it wouldn't be a discovery. It would be a received idea."

"Our worst enemy, huh?"

"That's right." Then releasing her and stepping back, putting his hands in his pockets, he asked, "Speaking of Wright, did he give you the contract?"

Julie smiled at the pun. "Yeah, he did. Is he in on this too?"

"Are *you* crazy?" asked Conner with a smirk.

"Not at all."

"Okay, then," said Conner, ignoring the question of

Wright's involvement, "you come back to class tomorrow, and we'll let things ride. I don't think anybody will object too much. Just remember, though, if anybody asks anything, tell them you're on the contract. Don't give everything away yet. Maybe we can still salvage the truth."

"Seriously?" Julie asked, startled by Mr. Conner's audacity, the cruelty of his expecting her to continue living the role that had brought her, angry and tearful, to him in the first place.

"Uh-huh," said Conner. "I'd like to think this wasn't all for nothing. I mean, you've played your part so well. You deserve something more than what you're feeling now."

"I don't want to go on with it. I want out. I've had enough excitement, okay?"

He looked at her for a long while, as though he were giving her a last chance to change her mind. Julie ignored his cue.

"Is that really the way you want it, Julie?"

"That's the way I want it."

Conner offered a smile, but it was ragged at the edges. He waited while she gathered up her books and walked her to the door. Before she could leave he said, "Just the excitement of being in my class is enough for you, huh?"

"It'll have to do, I guess."

"It will, then," he said, giving her another of his lingering knowing smiles.

Grimacing, Julie left the room.

CHAPTER
9

When Julie walked into class on Friday, she felt as though she'd been gone for two weeks, not just the two days of her actual "unexcused absence." After sitting down, she scanned the group. Only a few students returned her look. Most smiled—not maliciously, but knowingly, like Mr. Conner. Julie did her best to stifle her paranoia. She knew she had to be careful, do nothing without thinking first. After all, she was "on the contract," so one misstep would cost her everything. And she knew Mr. Conner wouldn't intercede to save her if she messed up.

The class hour began ominously with a tongue-lashing from Conner for the generally poor quality of the papers he'd just graded.

"What am I supposed to do with stuff like this?" he asked, waving the bundle of folded essays at the group.

"Roll 'em and smoke 'em," mumbled Kevin Ellison.

Julie couldn't help herself. She let out a coughing laugh.

Conner glared at her. "Is it so comical, Miss Lamar? I wouldn't think it could be, especially for someone in your . . . delicate condition."

Julie heard snickering from somewhere behind her but didn't dare turn around. "No," she said, staring down at her notebook, fearful the end was near.

"No," said Conner. "No, it isn't the least bit comical, is it. You people have supposedly been working in this class for nearly a quarter, and less than a quarter of you seem to be getting the gist of my expectations."

Julie was thrilled that Conner had returned so quickly to group condemnation. She thought maybe she'd lucked out for once.

"So for the rest of this hour," Conner continued, "I want you to look at an article that recently appeared in a professional journal. Read it carefully and then write at least a two-page response in which you relate the thrust of the piece to our objectives as a group and to your objectives as individual students of writing."

With that, Conner began handing out the photocopied article. By now the class was so anxious that no one dared to speak, to ask questions, to request clarification of the directions.

Julie examined her copy of the article. From even a cursory reading the message was clear: Language and outlook and identity are all related, the author argued. When we use language thoughtfully and imaginatively we become "genuinely creative," for in changing how we name what we see, we change what we see and who we are. This idea, Julie remembered, had been Conner's theme on the first day of class, the day when almost everybody was preoccupied with checking out who had gotten more beautiful or handsome, taller or stronger, over the summer. Julie had been listening to him.

The group worked quietly all hour. Mr. Conner sat behind his desk at the front of the room, his head bent over another class's essays. His face was expressionless. His right hand, however, the hand holding his weapon, a red felt-tip marking pen, was tense. It was ready to let blood, to cut into a sentence or paragraph that suffered from "prefabricated phrases" or "derivative, easy abstractions" or "careless and annoying mechanical errors" or a host of other pet objections. He did read their essays carefully. He did take their work seriously, thought Julie. You had to give him credit for that.

Julie completed her two pages of analysis, comparison, and contrast three minutes before the class period ended. When she had finished proofreading her essay, she checked to see if anyone else was done. To her amazement, only half a dozen of her classmates were still writing. The others sat there glancing furtively at one another.

The next time Julie looked at the clock, there were thirty seconds of class. She was curious as to why Conner hadn't called in their papers, along with his precious article—"I only have twenty-five of these, people, so don't do anything . . . *unnatural* to them, okay?" he'd said. Suddenly, twenty seconds before the bell, Julie heard a loud rhythmic shuffling, which meant everybody was doing something at once. All of the other students in the room grabbed their Warriner's grammar books, stood up, cocked their arms, and took aim at Conner.

As this happened, Conner lifted his head, an expression of irritation and confusion screwing up his normally even features. Then, as his eyes widened with comprehension, the rest of the class yelled *"For Julie!"* in unison and hurled their books at Conner.

"No!" Julie screamed, but she was too late.

Conner took three or four direct hits on his chest and head before sliding down behind his desk, seeking cover in the cubbyhole beneath it. Meanwhile, the books continued to crash loudly off the metal sheeting around the desk. Some books were thrown so hard they dented the desk front and sounded like exploding artillery shells.

As the mob stampeded for the door, pulling Julie along with it, she looked back just in time to see Kevin Ellison and three other guys take armloads of hardcover dictionaries from the nearby shelves and dump them all around Conner's desk, burying him, walling him in.

Julie fought against the laughing, catcalling, surging crowd. She was afraid Conner might be hurt. She had pushed her way to within a few steps of his desk when she heard him laughing hysterically from underneath it, still completely entombed. *"Good show!"* he was yelling over and over.

Julie turned and rushed out of the room, slamming the door shut behind her, certain now that he no longer cared about who she was or what she felt.

It wasn't until lunch that Julie was able to discuss what had happened with anybody. She was something more than shocked when all her friends began congratulating *her* for masterminding the rebel attack on Conner, the terrorist "book bombing."

"Way to kick his conceited ass!" thundered Gail, laughing her deep, harsh laugh, clapping Julie on the back so hard she spilled her forkful of peas.

"Yeah, Julie, you've got guts, all right," added Mary Artis.

"But I had nothing to do with it. Nothing!" Julie protested.

"Sure, sure," said Toby Eckerholm, Mary Artis's cerebral boyfriend. "If that's the official word, it's okay with us. Hey, don't worry. Your secret's safe."

At that point Julie realized it was useless to deny anything anymore. But she wasn't about to let herself get trapped again in a plot hatched by someone else, some unknown quantity. She finished her lunch and hurried to the senior wing, so called because it was where the seniors had their lockers. For once she was lucky. She found him there, dialing his combination, talking to a buddy. As she approached, the other guy wandered off.

"Kevin," said Julie. Kevin Ellison turned and smiled. "Yeah?"

"Whose idea was it to throw the books?"

"Yours, huh? You showed us the way."

"Seriously."

"Look, we wanted to get him," Kevin answered intensely. "Not just for you, either. For everything. For the way he acts. He's a jerk. He had it coming."

"But who organized it?"

"Don't ask me."

"You don't know?!"

"Uh-uh. And it's better that way, huh? Like everybody else, I found a piece of paper in my notebook yesterday. Other people found 'em in their lockers first thing this morning. We just assumed you put 'em there."

"What did it say? You still have it?"

"Naw, we all trashed 'em. It was just a line anyway, typed. It said, 'Friday, Conner, twenty seconds to go, stand up, yell FOR JULIE, throw WARRINERS.' "

"And nobody wants credit?" asked Julie.

"Strange, right? Considering what a helluva good idea it was. Made my day, you know? I mean, you see him hit the dirt? It was war, man—*ambush*!" Kevin's eyes glittered.

Realizing that Kevin had told her everything he knew,

she smiled, said "Thanks," and walked away before he could reply. She spent the last hours of the academic day being pointed at by underclassmen, hearing animated conversations start every time she passed through the clogged hallways. She waited glumly for the disciplinary ax of Vice-Principal Wright to fall and cut her off from college prep writing.

By day's end, though, she still hadn't seen the office aide. She dared to think she was safe. The smart thing would have been to go directly home after school and answer Mr. Wright's questions later, if ever. But lately Julie hadn't always been doing the smart or sensible thing. Instead she decided to face Conner for what she knew was the last time. Somehow it would all end today. She was convinced of it. For she knew now just how it was . . . and who had made it that way. What she still didn't know was why—exactly why.

After school she didn't even stop at her locker to drop off her books, but raced up to his room to keep him from escaping. She was determined not to let him get away without answering some questions. She'd been through enough. She had something to say to him and she would say it, whatever the cost. And he would listen.

She came striding into his room, shutting the door with a bang. He winced visibly at the noise.

"What the hell is going on?" she asked.

He looked at her blandly, his lips slightly parted.

"You set me up, didn't you?" she said. "Right from the start! Just to amuse yourself! Right? *Right?*" She was yelling now and didn't care. "You even set up that scene today, didn't you?"

Once again, as always, his flawless self-possession, his impeccable composure made her feel silly for having come on so strong. She'd caught him in the middle of grading papers, and he slowly, carefully recapped his pen, making her wait for an answer.

"Is it really that simple, Julie?" he asked quietly. "Is that the best you can do?"

She refused to comment, to get caught up in another scene.

"Sometimes things happen," Conner said ambiguously.

"But this time, today, in class, you *made* it happen. That's what I think."

"People can't be made vicious and violent by a mere suggestion. Can they?"

"Okay, did you *suggest* it, then?" Julie wasn't going to let the issue die. She wanted Conner to admit his involvement in the incident, to admit he instigated it, and in so doing, betrayed her. "Did you?" she repeated.

There was a long pause. Finally he said, "In the end the truth shall be revealed, and—"

Juile cut in, "This *is* the end! Can't you see that?"

"Is it?"

"Did you?"

"Did I what?"

"Oh c'*mon!*" said Julie, getting angrier. "Just answer me straight for once. Did you send out the little instruction slips to everybody?"

"There's a network of skilled operatives here who—"

"And that phone call the other night! That was you, too!"

"There is a network of operatives here and—"

"Give up!" Julie shouted. In frustration she looked away. Her anger was all she had at the moment, and she wanted to hang on to it. She scanned the room, noting that everything had been put back in perfect order. Even the books were once again neatly stacked on a table near the far wall.

"You called this a morality play," she said quickly, her voice thick with emotion. "A way of discovering the truth, a revealing experiment."

"Wasn't it?"

"Maybe from your warped perspective."

Again he paused before responding. "Is that all you're going to do with this experience?"

"What's that?"

"Use it as an excuse to call me names? Make irrelevant accusations?"

"I trusted you," she said. "Doesn't that mean anything?"

"Why did you trust me?"

"Because . . ."

It soon became clear she couldn't think of a single reason that didn't sound predictable or shallow. She had trusted him because he seemed so different, so special, so aware of her. She trusted him because he gave her what her father didn't or couldn't—time. Conner was accessible. Hadn't he spent hours with her, just talking to her, making her feel, day after day, like she was the most interesting person he'd met in a decade? Or was that too part of an elaborate facade?

"I don't know what's true anymore," she said.

"Why not?"

"Because you lied to me."

"Did I?"

"Yes! You've said lots of things that weren't true."

"Like?"

"I asked you if I'd get more detention."

"Did you?"

"You tried to get me kicked out of class!"

"Is that detention?"

She glared at him, quivering now with rage. "Who are you?" she yelled, unable to keep her anger and frustration in check, fed up with his glibness. "Okay, okay," she said quickly, trying to regain her self-control. "Who are you?" she asked more calmly.

When he didn't answer, she stood up to leave, fumbling with her books, dropping one of them. She felt clumsy, helpless, embarrassed, and vulnerable. She bent down, retrieved the book, and tried again to leave. But this time Conner reached over and grabbed her forearm and held it firmly.

"Let go!" she cried. "Let go of me!"

"Don't leave, Julie," he said soothingly. "Don't quit now."

She struggled against his grip, but he held fast. She didn't want to jerk herself away and risk spilling her books another time.

"Stay," he said. "Please."

"Why should I?"

"Because we're getting to the heart of the matter. I want to tell you about something now that you couldn't have understood or appreciated a week ago."

"Another lie? Another psychodrama?"

"You be the judge."

She refused to say more, refused even to look at him.

"If I let go, will you stay?"

She gave a barely perceptible nod and Conner released her.

"I want to tell you about something that happened a long, long time ago, something important. Will you try to listen carefully?"

95

Julie said, "Okay."

Conner sat back, took a deep breath, expelled it, and stared down at his desk and his loosely fisted hands. "It's about the picture," he said.

"The one in your briefcase?" she asked softly.

"Yes."

CHAPTER
10

At last he turned to meet her gaze. For once he looked doubtful. "Yes," he repeated. "It's about that picture." He let another moment pass. "This is it, Julie," he said, surprising her. "I don't think I'll get another chance to do this. There won't ever be another person like you . . . who's *ready* for it. It's like you arrived just when I most needed someone to listen." His eyes wavered again, then hardened with resolve.

"The other guy in the picture," Conner began, staring at the back wall, "was my best friend in high school."

He spoke in a controlled monotone as if he'd been saying the words to himself over and over. "After graduation, we both entered the university, but by spring we both knew we weren't ready for the discipline of college. And we knew the Vietnam War wouldn't be over even if we stayed in school three more years to avoid it. So we did the dumbest thing possible. We volunteered for the draft. The Army promised us we'd be together from boot camp on. I was glad of that. My friend was special. He had it all—talent, intelligence, decency. I was much more impulsive. I talked him into joining the Army. That was my first betrayal.

"After boot camp, we took infantry training. Then we were sent to Nam for the thirteen-month Grand Tour. We were in the same company, same platoon, same squad even. We were stationed at Phu Bai in I Corps, the northernmost military zone. At first our squad drew only perimeter guard duty. We didn't pull any bush patrol for the first few weeks in-country. Then one day we got called in. A captain told us we were going to be briefed that evening for an important reconnaissance mission, a 'sneak-and-peak' job.

"The night that changed everything for us was hot and humid and ugly. The ten of us who met with the captain learned we'd be going out immediately by twos on night patrol. Our objective was to ascertain enemy strength in an area northwest of our fire base. There was a river our troops would have to cross when they moved northwest to assemble for a major offensive, a huge search-and-destroy *pervertathon*. Supposedly it was a division-sized operation, so we were responsible for guaranteeing the safety of nearly twenty-five hundred men. The river our troops would cross was shallow, but it was wide enough to leave them helpless and vulnerable if they got caught there by the VC or NVA.

"My friend and I were the first twosome to leave. We had orders to cover the far sector, the one billed as 'least likely to contain enemy troops.' We blessed our luck. Our only specific task was to check out a deserted VC base camp.

"At dusk we got ready. Before leaving, we did every-thing that real jungle warriors should do. We blackened our faces with charcoal and shoe polish. We taped down anything on our uniforms or weapons that rattled and could give us away. We sprayed ourselves with insect re-pellent even though we knew it was useless against those big Nam bugs. The whole time we were outfitting our-selves, we never thought to ask why they'd send a couple of cherries like us on this mission. We were newcomers, green. And this patrol seemed so crucial.

"We hiked out into the bush so scared we couldn't even talk. The night was dark and moonless, hot and still. The air was so heavy and wet the jungle smelled like a damp cellar. In five minutes I was sweat-soaked.

"We were supposed to cross a ridge and then work our way through the valley on the other side. At first, going up the ridge was easy. There was a trail running through the thick bamboo forest. We'd been told to follow it even though most of the trails in the zone were mined. We stayed on it anyway until we found an opening to the valley. Then we slid down into the wet, mucky ravine.

"Bent double, we tried to step lightly through the dense undergrowth, but the muddy valley floor sucked at our boots. It felt like quicksand. The air in the valley smelled of rotting trees and plants, and then the mosquitoes found us.

"The base camp we were looking for was still hours away. Our pace was very slow. About halfway there my friend slipped in the mud and stumbled down a gully, made a lot of noise. I dove for cover, sure we'd be caught. Neither of us could see a thing, and that made us panic. The still-ness was unreal. Lying there in that stinking red mud, I felt like I was crawling through a sewer. I could hardly breathe.

"Finally we decided it was safe to go on. We'd been

told the camp was up in the cliffs on the other side of the valley. The jungle growth surrounding the complex of caves and bunkers camouflaged it so well that to see anything we had to get close. By then I'd lost all track of time.

"We began working toward a vantage point on the far ridge. Along the way, all we thought about were trip wires and booby traps and pongee pits. Scaling this ridge was a lot harder. The slope quickly became so steep we had to climb hand over hand, grabbing roots. At the top we stumbled into a thorn patch and got cut up even more. Suddenly my friend shushed me. He pointed down the ridge line. We saw cooking fires. The camp was hardly deserted.

"We decided to move a little closer. I crawled forward, fighting the need to hurry up and get things over with. As we pulled ourselves through the mud, we could hear things slithering in the underbrush. We rose slightly to look at the complex. I thought I saw enough men in the shadows to make up a battalion. There seemed to be hundreds.

"We spotted both VC and NVA soldiers. Some were cleaning weapons, others were packing gear. We wanted to hurry back to our lines with the information. But just as we turned to go, four or five VC popped up from nowhere and jammed their AK-47's into the backs of our necks. I never heard a thing until they jumped us. It was like they'd been there all the time.

"They pushed us facedown in the mud. They took our guns and tied our arms together behind our backs. Then they pulled us to our feet and blindfolded us. In silence they led us down a trail, but they didn't take us to the camp. Instead we went on a jungle march. Hours later we stopped and they took off our blindfolds. I saw we were near a large bunker. They took us inside. The walls were solid concrete except for some machine-gun slits. The only light came from a smoky kerosene lamp. I looked at my friend. Like me he was hot, wet, tired, dirty, and scared.

"Before I had time to see any more, they undid my arms and threw me into a wooden chair at one end of the room. They quickly retied my arms and legs to the arms and legs of the chair. I watched them strap my friend into a chair fixed against the opposite wall. We stared at each other across the ten-foot space separating us. His eyes were wide and blank. He was terrified.

"Next they brought in a little gasoline generator and set it down between us. I didn't know that's what it was until they started tearing open my friend's clothes. They taped electrical wires to him, all over his body. He tried to resist, but it was useless. He was tied too tightly.

"I screamed something, I don't remember what. Swore maybe. But before I could yell again, somebody came out of the shadows and chopped me in the throat. I started choking and gagging. I couldn't see for a few seconds. Everything went red.

"When they finished with my friend, they started the generator. The noise was deafening. I knew then we were far from American lines. The VC and NVA were a lot of things, but they weren't stupid. They'd never make so much noise if it left them vulnerable.

"After warming up the generator, one of them took out a little control box with half a dozen buttons on it. He looked at me and smiled. He raised his eyebrows and nodded, extending the box to me, seeming to ask, 'Do you see now? Do you understand what's going to happen here?' Then he turned slowly to my friend and pushed the first button. The shock made him scream and grit his teeth. The convulsions slammed him back against the wall.

"The VC with the box turned to me again and smiled.

'Well, what do you think of that?' he seemed to say. Before I could react, three of them came at me, all hollering in Vietnamese, questioning me, I suppose. I couldn't understand a word, and I was too scared to talk or shout anything back. After fifteen or twenty seconds they stopped and signaled the man with the box. Again he hit the button and jolted my friend. Then I started screaming and swearing.

"They hit me with their fists and gun butts. I tried to topple myself into them. I wanted to hurt somebody before they finished me. And I had no doubt we'd be killed. But I couldn't budge. They held me firmly all around.

"My friend looked at me and begged with his eyes. He was pouring sweat. The room smelled horrible. He'd already rubbed away the skin where the ropes held him. He was bleeding from his nose and mouth. I wanted to say something to him, ask him what I should do. He sensed what I was thinking and started shaking his head. 'Nothing!' he was saying, 'Tell them nothing!'

"Suddenly the room went black. They'd hit me and then blindfolded me again. Now I was dizzy and the noise and smoke of the generator were making me sick. I threw up all over myself. But they kept at it, screaming questions and accusations point-blank in rapid-fire Vietnamese. Again when they stopped and I said nothing, there was a short pause before my friend started howling. He yelled for a long time. The generator kept hammering away and it didn't drown him out.

"I was struggling to hear all I could when one of the VC came close and said in very passable English, 'You like it better if we ask in your language, huh? You like that a little better, you Yankee bastard?' I didn't answer. 'You arrogant Yankee bastard, come here and don't know the language or the land or the history, and you expect to

102

defeat us?' Again I remained silent. I would say nothing.
The Code of Conduct. 'Okay, you stupid Yankee bastard,
now tell us where are the soldiers, the ARVN and Americans!' I shook my head. Three seconds later my friend
cried out. The VC asked, 'Are you a deserter, huh?' I yelled,
'No!' He said, 'No? But you do what a deserter does. You
run and let your comrade die, Yankee bastard. You don't
love your comrade. You don't even love yourself. That is
why we will win.' Then he bellowed, 'WHERE ARE THE
AMERICANS?' I knew as soon as I shook my head what
would happen, and it did. My friend's screams cut right
through me. I thought I was dying, not him. 'You stupid,
stupid Yankee bastard!' the VC yelled at me. Then he
slapped me across the face. He didn't punch me or club
me. He slapped me like you would a naughty, insolent
child. And that's when I saw it, the thing that made us
so different. If he was going to kill me, it wasn't because
I'd refused to tell him about the mission. He wanted me
dead because I had no imagination, I wouldn't think for
myself. He was genuinely disgusted with me for allowing
my friend to suffer, for not being smart enough or daring
enough to save him, for obeying our 'imperialist military
code,' for being loyal to an institutional ideal I'd been
fooled into believing was bigger than individual
loyalty.

"He slapped me again and again. Over and over we
went through the same ritual. He yelled questions at me,
I said nothing, and my friend screamed and screamed and
screamed. And all the while that damn generator kept
pounding, pounding, pounding. Then I broke.

"I howled and cried and cursed and fought against
the ropes. They jabbed and slapped me, and laughed at
me. And because I was still blindfolded, I couldn't tell
where the next punch was coming from. By then I was

barely conscious. Finally one of them hit me hard enough to knock me out.

"When I woke up I could smell the exhaust from the generator. It stung my broken, blood-clotted nose. Everything was quiet. I tried to call out, but my throat was so sore from being chopped and jabbed, from screaming, that I couldn't make a sound. I was lying sideways on the floor, still tied to the chair, still blindfolded. My head throbbed. I hurt everywhere. I tried to move and discovered that my fall had broken an arm of the chair. Soon I was able to work my right hand free. When I did, I tore off the blindfold and found the room, the bunker, completely empty. I'd been spared.

"It was then, just as I began wrestling with the other ropes, that the pain arced through my skull, shooting from side to side, base to top. I collapsed. When I came to, I reached up and felt my temple. My hair was matted and wet. My hand came away covered with blood. I'd been shot. Or shot at. If they were trying to execute me, they had done a lousy job.

"Eventually I could stay awake long enough to work myself out of the ropes. I was deep in enemy territory. I was completely unarmed. I was alone. And I'd lost, sacrificed, my best friend. To make his death meaningful, I had to get back to our lines as soon as possible and warn them about the enemy buildup. I stumbled out of the bunker into the heat, vowing to avenge my friend and win back my honor.

"I don't remember much about my escape. It was very hot and humid, so I tried to stay in the woods and heavy brush. I think I wandered around for a few days. I didn't see anybody, any villages, until the night I spotted a base camp. By then I didn't care whose camp it was. I was so hungry and thirsty and tired I'd tell anybody anything they wanted to hear just for a little rest. I never made it all the way in. I passed out on the perimeter wire. Thank God, I said when I woke up in an American field hospital." Conner looked at the floor. He seemed exhausted.

"But you were safe at least," said Julie, short of breath.

"Not exactly. They weren't through with me yet."

CHAPTER
11

"When I came to, my head was heavily bandaged. It seemed like I'd barely regained consciousness when the same captain who'd sent us out came in to question me. He began with 'Where'n hell have you been, soldier?' Before I could work up an answer, he said, 'You tell Charlie Cong about the operation? About moving the division across the river?'

"That question meant he knew I'd been captured and interrogated. He asked again, 'You tell 'em about the operation? C'mon, speak up.' Proudly I shook my head no. 'No, sir,' I whispered. 'No?' he yelled. 'No?' Then I said, 'I didn't talk, sir.' He let out a sigh, hung his head a second, grunted. Finally he said, 'Goddam you, can't you goddam grunts do any goddam thing right? Can't we count on anything anymore?' With that he turned around and started to leave.

"I was so stunned by his reaction I thought he'd mis-understood me. He was nearly out the door when I screamed 'I didn't talk! I didn't tell about the mission!' He came back to my bed, put his nose in my face, and snarled, 'You were *supposed* to talk, you stupid sonuvabitch.' Then he turned on his heel and went toward the door again. But he stopped short, looked over his shoulder at me, and said, 'Oh, almost forgot. Here's your medal . . . hero.' He tossed me a little plastic box with a purple heart in it. I never tried to catch it. I let it clatter onto the floor and left it there. I closed my eyes to keep anybody from seeing me cry. That's when I remembered to ask about my friend. I called out to the captain once more. He just kept walking, didn't even break stride."

Julie watched as Conner covered his exhausted face with his hands. Then, for the first time during the whole long, detailed narrative, Conner looked at her. He stared intensely and seemed about to say something else. She was nearly in shock herself, emotionally drained. She shared his hurt. She had never really believed that such things could happen to people, people you could meet and talk to. It was always somebody else's experience, something you read about in books or old magazines.

"They set me up, Julie," he said at last. "Both sides set me up. Can you imagine that? I couldn't. The Army sent me out there full of gung ho military idealism and phony information, hoping I'd get caught and spill what I knew to the VC. I mean, they were counting on us to do just that. And they were willing to sacrifice me to get their big body count for the week. But worse than anything that happened to me while I was captured, was finding out about my friend.

"He'd gotten back home, too. He was also crazier than hell. They put him in a psych ward in San Diego. An

American patrol found him wandering in the bush. The VC had disarmed and released him.

"When the VC caught us, they obviously knew exactly what we were, a couple of ignorant nobodies from nowhere who could at least amuse them for a while. And we were entertaining. From what I've learned, the VC only shocked my friend when I wasn't blindfolded. After that, once the blindfold went on, everything was staged. *Staged.* They held a gun to my friend's head and told him to scream on cue. They cocked and uncocked the trigger, terrified him.

"But what really put him over was having to sit there and watch me betray him for the sake of upholding a code that my own officer expected me to break. And all the while I resisted, they were telling my friend in English that I hated him and only loved killing, and soon I would kill him. And he believed that, I guess. All I could hear where his screams.

"So that night I was exposed. They showed me I was morally bankrupt and stood for nothing of value and was mortally stupid. And I was cut off forever from the only honest relationship I'd had to that point. *My* reaction to the truth I discovered in that field hospital was to develop an 'acute anxiety reaction' that led to a 'post-traumatic stress disorder.' Army jargon. When I was ready to leave the hospital, they didn't send me back to the War. They sent me back to the World, to a clinic in Seattle. I was released six months later, a 'whole man,' a 'solid citizen.' "

Conner's irony was so bitter it made Julie cringe.

She whispered, "Oh my God."

Conner focused on her, his eyes shining, his face ashen, his expression pleading for a response, a judgment, a justification. "I've never told anyone about this, never the whole story, all at once. Never straight."

That's when Julie suddenly understood what Conner

108

had been up to. She saw that he had been in *other* psychodramas—at least one other. But it was a play where the stakes were much higher than any she could imagine. And worse, he'd lost the game. They'd beaten him and taken away his friend, his self-respect, and nearly his sanity. And it had taken him years to win back some of what was lost.

In their psychodrama, she was obviously playing the part of Conner's younger self, Conner the soldier, the victim of a crazy, dirty war thousands of miles from home. One parallel detail after another flashed through her mind. She saw that like Conner she too had been put in a position where she had to choose and where her choices had consequences—major ones for her. She saw that the more difficult her choices had become, the more meaningless, even absurd they'd become, so that soon her choices appeared to have no influence on events in real life. But had they really been her choices?

Julie had also sacrificed friendships for a greater ideal, the trust she'd placed in a fantasy relationship, the one she never had with her father. And hers had been a blind trust. But Julie still wasn't able to see exactly what Conner wanted her to learn from the psychodrama. She knew what had happened and why it happened, but she wasn't sure yet what it all meant.

"Do you see the truth now?" asked Conner, startling her, breaking the spell.

"I see how what happened to you is like what's happening to me. But I don't know what to think about it."

"There are no easy answers, no formulas." He sat quietly a moment. "Do you trust me?" he blurted, jarring her again. "Still?"

"Yes," Julie said simply, without a second thought.

"How can you? Haven't I betrayed you too?"

"Have you?"

"What do you think? That's what's important."

"I feel confused, but not betrayed. Not now."

"But you did when you came in here, right?"

"Yes. I was mad. I thought you used me."

"Why aren't you upset now?"

"Because of what you told me about the war."

"The war," muttered Conner. "It's always *the war*. Here's a thought," he went on brightly. "What if I told you this whole Vietnam thing was a lie, another installment in the psychodrama?" His cold stare suggested she take him seriously.

Julie shuddered. Her mind started racing. "Was it?" she asked, her throat tight at the thought of being taken again.

"Was it?" Conner repeated.

Slowly, tentatively, she shook her head. Then she began turning it forcefully from side to side as if to say no, it simply *can't be* another lie. Just as quickly she stopped, and a little smile started to form.

"Why are you smiling?" Conner asked gently.

"Because I just thought of a line from a poem. It explains why I believe what you told me."

"What is it?"

" 'The heart knows.' "

"The heart knows what?"

"The truth."

"How can you say that?" prompted Conner.

"Because I want to say it. I decided to say it. The story's true, morally or something, whether it actually happened or not."

"So you've decided to trust me."

"Yes."

"Just as I decided to trust my captain?"

"Yes."

"What if I hadn't trusted anyone in the war? What if I hadn't decided to go one way or the other?"

"You'd be . . . lost."

"How?"

"You'd wind up doing what somebody else decided whether you knew it or not. You've got to choose. Otherwise you're lost."

"*Exactly*," Conner whispered, his gray eyes gleaming. "There are some things we should never give up, not if we're going to be free."

"I don't get it," Julie said.

"What don't you get?"

"Shouldn't I trust anyone now, anyone but you?"

"Never trust blindly. To live well you must learn to choose well, and to do that, you must be careful. You must know what you want and what it costs and what you're willing to pay. Freedom and truth, they're never gifts."

"What if the truth hurts?"

"Nothing hurts more than doing nothing."

"I know."

"Life is difficult," said Conner. "But also rich. Varied and rich. And you are especially well equipped to perceive and appreciate its richness. But you'll be tempted many times to become unreflective, blindly accepting—a passive victim. You can't allow that."

Julie was stunned by Conner's words and the intense look on his face. She knew that at this moment he meant absolutely every word he said, that all pretenses, all roles, all masks had been put aside. She felt this conversation justified all she'd been through. Conner had shared with her the most valuable thing he possessed: a life secret, an ultimate insight. In the only way he could, through the action of the psychodrama, he had enabled her to learn his greatest lesson.

She looked up and found Conner studying her. "You're gonna do okay," he said.

She took a deep breath, then asked, "Now what?"

"We've got to get back to normal. First I should bring everyone back from the dead. That'll be on Monday."

"Me too?"

"You especially."

"And then?"

"And then no more psychodramas."

"How can you say that? You're always setting things in motion."

"What I meant was, the next time you see me masking it in class, the role-playing will be mere escapism."

"Oh, sure."

"You understand how it is," he said.

Julie replied, "The heart knows."

"I guess it does at that."

"It's a wonderful feeling," said Julie, getting up to leave.

"What?"

"To have survived."

Conner nodded silently, reached over to touch her hand in parting. As he did so, she felt him slip, felt him surrender, quietly giving up the torment of memory. And for one bright moment Julie knew everything was clear between them at last.

CHAPTER
12

Before third hour the follow-
ing Monday, Julie and the rest of the class found themselves
locked out of Conner's room. After the last bell had rung,
the students began joking uneasily about what Conner was
up to now.

"Could be he wants us to bring notes from our mom-
mies and daddies saying we're so sorry."

"Fat chance."

"No way, Ray."

Suddenly the door flew open and there was Conner
dressed as a doctor with a long white lab coat covering
his blue shirt, regimental tie, and gray slacks. A stethoscope
hung around his neck. In his left hand he held a clipboard,
in his right a ballpoint pen.

"Next!" he called.

The students looked at one another, shrugged, and

shuffled silently past Conner and into the room. As they moved toward their desks, they saw Conner had already placed their Warriner's books over a sheet of paper in the middle of each desktop. Julie smiled when she discovered that the paper was the contract. Conner was putting the entire class "on the contract." Naturally he had personalized the document. At the top of the sheet he'd added the following paragraph:

On Friday the fifteenth I was seized by a violently insane impulse. I was not myself. I was deranged. I didn't mean to do what I did. I regret it and wish to forget it. I want my brains unscrambled, my head screwed on straight, my act together. I want to be normal again, honest. But you never know. I could slip once more into the bottomless pit of madness. So to discipline myself and give you "assurances," I want to sign this pledge of cooperation. I want to fit into the program here. I want to be happy. I want to live in peace.

Meanwhile, Conner was writing something on the blackboard. He still hadn't said anything. When he was finished and had replaced the chalk in the tray and seated himself behind his desk, Julie read what he'd written:

THIS IS A MERCIFUL INSTITUTION. I AM NOT A VINDICTIVE PERSON. I ASSUME YOU ARE RATIONAL. INSANITY IS IN THE EYES OF THE BEHOLDER, AFTER ALL. SO NOW YOU HAVE A REASONABLE CHOICE TO MAKE. YOU MAY:

1. SIGN AND SURVIVE
OR
2. WRITE NO AND GO.

Still silent, Conner stared down at the clipboard on his desk and waited for the students to choose. Slowly, reluctantly, inevitably, everyone signed the form and sent it up to a row captain. It wasn't until Julie had handed in her behavior contract (her second in a week) that she noticed the little slip of blue paper inside her grammar book. She slid it out. On it Mr. Conner had typed a couplet. It read:

There is no end to this array,
No final curtain for our play.

During the rest of the hour the class worked on several sentence-styling exercises Conner had mutely handed to them. No one asked a question or made a dull remark. No one dared to. At the end of the morguelike session, everyone filed quietly out, leaving the completed exercises on Conner's desk.

After school Julie went back to Conner's room, found him packing his briefcase. She stepped in and said, "No final curtain?"

He looked up. "It just goes on and on," he said.

Julie said, "Yeah. I kind of thought it would."